BAHAMIAN ESCAPADE

ADVENTURE IN THE ABACOS, ELEUTHERA AND EXUMA ISLANDS

Catherine Kent Walker

"This is my command - be strong and courageous! Do not be afraid or discouraged. For the LORD your God is with you wherever you go."

— Joshua 1:9 (NLT)

CONTENTS

CHAPTER 1

The Interview

"I cannot believe it! I am going to crew on a sailboat this summer!" I said to myself as I reviewed my checklist of items to pack. I thought about the events leading up to this moment. Wading through the week of final exams during my sophomore year at Emory University, I took a break and visited the Student Center. Just inside the foyer stood a bulletin board perched atop a metal easel with want ads posting part-time jobs. I stopped, browsing the typical employment opportunities that dotted the cork board. "Hmm, secretaries, sales clerks, dog sitters, domestic work – boring," I read out loud. My gaze fell upon a flyer searching for students interested in learning to sail. "Now this looks interesting," I spoke to the air. Looking into my purse, I grabbed a pen, found an old sales receipt and jotted down the phone number.

The next afternoon, I had an interview with Harvey Merritt at his home in Decatur – not far from campus. I maneuvered my car along the winding driveway through a canopy of trees that gave way to a beautifully manicured lawn. I thought, for a moment, that I had entered a time warp and was approaching Tara. Looming ahead was a massive, two-story mansion with white columns lining the front porch. I parked my car in front of the adjoining three-car garage. I folded down the visor and checked myself in the mirror. I combed my brown hair, applied a fresh coat of lip gloss and exited my car advancing to the front door. I rang the doorbell and momentarily, a stately gentleman in a dark suit opened the door. "Hello, I am Aspen Blair. You must be Mr. Merritt," I said as I extended my hand.

"My name is Jones, Mr. Merritt's butler," he smiled. "Mr. Merritt is expecting you." Jones bowed and motioned with his right hand for me to enter the foyer. "This way, please," he added. I withdrew my hand and followed Jones through a lavish living room. The walls were taupe with white trim. A large white sofa, with matching recliners, rested under the windows that faced the front porch. Jones gestured for me to sit down. "Mr. Merritt will be with you shortly." He bowed again and left the room. Opposite this furniture was the largest big-screen television that I had ever seen. A black baby grand piano was on display in the far right corner next to a recessed bookcase. "I could live in a house like this," I thought. I retrieved my cell phone from my purse and no sooner than I had started to play a game, a well-tanned, balding, slender man walked into the room.

"Good afternoon. I am Harvey Merritt," he said, advancing towards the couch.

I arose and responded, "I am Aspen Blair; pleased to meet you, Mr. Merritt." He was wearing a white short-sleeved shirt and olive shorts – complete with boat shoes.

"Please call me Harvey. Shall we have a seat?"

I obeyed and Mr. Merritt sat down on the opposite end of the sofa. About that time, Jones returned with a tray containing a pitcher of ice water with sliced lime wedges and two glasses. "May I offer you some refreshment?" Jones asked me.

"Yes, thank you." Jones placed the tray on the coffee table, poured and handed a drink to me and Mr. Merritt. He quietly retreated to the hallway.

"I would like to tell you a little about myself," Harvey began. "I am a retired IBM executive. My wife Carol is a high school teacher who is nearing retirement. We are avid weekend boaters. I secretly bought a 44-foot catamaran as her retirement gift. We have often discussed living on a boat and sailing in the Bahamas. A friend of mine, Buddy Sharp, has agreed to captain the boat. Being an Emory alumnus, I decided to hire several college students as crew. My scheme is for Buddy and his crew to sail the vessel to a marina at Georgetown in the Exuma Islands. I am going to tell my wife that I rented a sailboat for a week's vacation in the Bahamas in celebration of her retirement. I sure hope she likes the boat because, on our first day, I will reveal my surprise!"

"Wow!" I exclaimed. "That is so romantic. Exactly where is Georgetown?"

Harvey explained, "It is the capital of the Exumas and in Great Exuma Island. Here, let me show you on this globe."

We walked over to the bookcase where the globe was shelved.

Harvey began, "Here is Florida and, over here, are the Northern Abaco Islands. Eleuthera is a little further south, and below that are the Exuma Islands. As you see here, Andros and Bimini are closer to the coast of Florida. What is called the 'tongue of the ocean' separates Andros and Bimini from Eleuthera and the Exuma Islands."

"Looks like quite an adventure to me!" I exclaimed.

"Aspen, do you have any boating experience?"

"I have been on small sailboats on Lake Lanier. I know how to steer a ski boat, sailed on a Hobie Cat, can drive a jet ski and passed a safe boating course," I said enthusiastically. "My parents are retired from the Coast Guard Auxiliary, and I learned a lot from them."

Harvey replied, "Well, you are the first student I have interviewed who has any knowledge about handling a boat. There is a big difference between the lake and the open sea. For one thing, there are no sea or wind currents to deal with on inland lakes."

"Where is the sailboat now?"

"She is docked at a marina in St. Marys, Georgia." Harvey summoned Jones. "Jones, will you bring me the laptop in my study, please?"

Appearing at the doorway, Jones replied, "Certainly, sir." Then he disappeared, shortly returning into the room, and handed Harvey his computer.

"Thank you, Jones," Harvey said. Jones acknowledged his remark with a slight bow and silently exited the room. As Harvey was powering up his laptop, he said, "Let me show you some pictures of my boat." I scooted over toward the center of the couch, and he placed his computer in the center of the table. He positioned the screen to my attention.

Harvey described the various photos of his magnificent yacht. I learned that a catamaran consists of two parallel hulls that support the frame that is 26 feet in width and 44 feet in length. Forward from the cabin to the bow stretches a net called a trampoline connected to the two pontoons. A flybridge perches atop the structure with a 74-foot mast. The aft davits supports a 12-foot dinghy. Atop the roof are solar panels and two wind generators.

"Wow! It's beautiful!" I exclaimed. "How many people can live on the boat?"

"There are three cabins. Buddy will stay in the owner's suite which is the cabin on the starboard or right side. The two crew members will have their own cabin on the port or left side."

Harvey continued our interview and allowed me time to ask any more questions. I asked, "What are the wages?"

"One hundred dollars a day. Depending on the weather, it will probably take a month to get to Georgetown. You will get $1,000 up front for your travel expenses and receive the balance upon returning home, including the cost of your airfare."

After some more discussion, Harvey said, "Aspen, you seem to be a capable, young lady. Would you like the job?"

"It sounds wonderful. I would like to discuss it with my parents first. Could I call you with my decision tomorrow?"

"Certainly," Harvey replied. "I will be available all day."

I arose from the couch and said, "It is certainly nice to meet you, Harvey."

Harvey stood as well, shaking my hand, "It has been my pleasure." He summoned Jones who escorted me to the door.

I returned to my dorm room, packed my things and drove home. Mom and Dad lived about one hour away in North Georgia. Dad was a retired Professor of Theology and taught a few classes at a local community college. Mom kept busy with housekeeping and church ministries. My brother Austin lived in Virginia.

Last year, my parents and I visited my brother who found some old family letters. In 1800, one of our ancestors, Thomas Newell, was falsely accused of multiple murders due to a collapsed mine shaft and robbed of his inheritance in England. He fled to America to avoid prison. I found a letter written by Timothy Sutton, brother of the man who committed the crimes. Inside the envelope was a key to a spar box that Timothy constructed. There he hid the stolen money after the death of his brother.

My parents and I went to England. That is where I met Tyler Dent at the Mining Museum. I learned that fabrication of spar boxes was a local art exclusively made by lead miners. Nature scenes were composed of colorful minerals from the mines, including feldspar, and prompted the name of the spar box. We formed a friendship; and together we found the spar box and Thomas's inheritance, which were 47 gold sovereigns. I sold them at auction, which afforded enough money to pay for my tuition; and I invested the rest. I kept one gold coin as a memento and had a necklace made for it. Tyler's Uncle Allen was serving time in prison for attempting to steal the gold coins, resisting arrest – not to mention threatening me and locking me and Tyler in a closet.

Tyler, having just graduated from his university with a degree in museum history and with his work at the Mining Museum, was offered a job at the Atlanta Science Center, not far from Emory University. I only had two years left before graduation.

My dad and Harvey had been classmates at Emory. Dad had not seen him for years. After talking to him, Dad gave his approval for me to take the job. Harvey had been unable to find another student suitable for crew. I talked to Tyler about the job; he thought it was a grand idea. He also had lots of vacation time. Harvey was quite impressed with Tyler and offered him the position of the second crew member. I was thrilled. I had not been able to see much of Tyler this year with his busy schedule at the Atlanta Science Center and my class schedule.

The next morning, I called Harvey. His butler, Jones, answered, "Merritt residence."

"Good morning, Jones," I replied. "May I speak to Harvey, please?"

"Certainly, Miss Aspen. May I place you on hold for a few seconds?"

"Of course," I said; and moments later, Harvey picked up the phone.

"Hello, Aspen. Good to hear from you. Have you made a decision?"

I responded, "Yes sir, Tyler and I accept the positions as crew."

"Splendid! Buddy lives in Florida now and will arrive at St. Marys within the week. I have given him a checklist to make sure the boat is ready to set sail, as well as a list of needed supplies. The sooner ya'll arrive, the better. That way Buddy will have time to familiarize you with the boat and teach you a few tips about sailing. That also will give you time to stock up the galley or, should I say, the kitchen," Harvey added. "When are you and Tyler planning to drive to the coast?"

"I think we should be able to leave by the end of the week – Thursday or Friday," I answered.

"That will be fine," Harvey said. "Let me give you Buddy's mobile number, and I will share your mobile number with Buddy. I have your checks ready. Just drop by the house before you leave. I have instructed Jones to give them to you. Bye for now, and I will pray for safe travel for you all."

I only had a few items left to buy and pack my bags. All that was left to do was to reserve a rental car.

CHAPTER 2

St. Marys, Georgia

Mom and Dad traveled to Atlanta to pick up the rest of the stuff from my dorm room, and we spent the night at a motel close to the rental car business. Tyler had an apartment near Emory and had a neighbor drop him off to pick up our rental car, and we met him there. Tyler had his black hair cut short for the summer. His blue eyes still mesmerized me since we had first met. We said our goodbyes to my parents and threw our bags into the trunk – excited about our new adventure.

The drive to St. Marys was about six hours away. Much of the drive was on two-lane roads that went through several small towns. One of the towns that we traveled through was Wrens, Georgia. "Tyler," I asked, "do you like nuts?"

"Nutty people or nuts you eat?" he quipped.

I gave him a courtesy laugh and replied, "There is a store there called The Orchards. Mom told me it was famous for a store that sells all kinds of gourmet nuts and gifts."

Tyler responded, "Sounds like a great place to take a break!"

Being the navigator for the trip, I put the address in the GPS. The store was on the main road on which we were traveling and convenient to stop there. We purchased a bag of walnuts and pecans and treated ourselves to some praline pecan candy. As we were leaving, I said, "These nuts will come in as a handy and healthy snack on the boat. On the way home, let's stop again and pick up some walnuts and pecans for Mom."

Tyler added, "Yes, and we can buy more to stock our cabinets when we get back to Atlanta."

We were not far from Interstate-16, which intersected with Interstate-95. Once on I-95, we passed exits for Savannah, Jekyll and St. Simon's Islands and Brunswick. I remember reading a poem by Sidney Lanier entitled, "The Marshes of Glynn," which was about the salt marshes in Brunswick, in Glynn County. We were only an hour away from St. Marys.

"What's that smell?" Tyler asked as he scrunched his nose.

"That is the salt air from the marshes." When I was younger, my parents had taken us on vacation to St. Simons and Jekyll Islands, and I remembered that smell.

Tyler said, "Well, I don't like it."

I replied, "You had better get used to it. There are marshes in St. Marys."

It wasn't long before we saw the exit to Kingsland and St. Marys. "Tyler, did you know there was a nuclear submarine base in Kingsland?"

"No, I did not," he answered. "How do you know so much?"

"I did some research of the area a couple of days ago. Cumberland

Island is nearby St. Marys. That is where John Kennedy Jr. was married to Carolyn Bessette."

Tyler said, "My, my, you are a plethora of information!"

St. Marys was about six miles from the exit ramp. Highway 40 took us through the main town of St. Marys before reaching the historic section which dead-ended at a beautiful park and pavilion. "I'll text Buddy, tell him we are here and ask him where to park." Several minutes later, I read Buddy's text, "Drive to the lower end of the parking area and find a place on that side. I will walk down the ramp and meet you. I am wearing a beige floppy hat. What color is your car?"

I texted back, "We are in a red SUV. See you soon!" Then I said to Tyler while pointing to a parking spot, "Tyler, park over there; Buddy is coming to meet us." We found an empty parking spot. There was a seafood restaurant a few yards down the street. We could see boat docks in the distance and a long ramp that crossed over marshland to the park. While waiting, we heard a horn sound and noticed that a ferry boat

Sunset at St. Marys River basin, St Marys, Georgia

was slowing down to dock at a terminal. "This must be the Cumberland Island Ferry," I exclaimed, seeing people disembarking and walking through the park to their cars. "This is the highlight of the town," Tyler said. Because of the distractions, we were unaware that Buddy was approaching our car until he knocked on my window. I almost jumped out of my seat! Buddy appeared to be about the same height as my dad – around 6 feet tall. I guessed his age to be around 40 years old – give or take. He wore a short-sleeved blue shirt, with various fish, and cargo pants. His arms were muscular. Buddy had brown, wavy hair.

"Buddy!" I got out of the car. "I'm Aspen Blair," and as Tyler came around the front of the car, I said, "and this is Tyler Dent."

"So nice to finally meet you in person! I have heard a lot of great things about you from Harvey." Buddy continued, "I thought we might have dinner at one of the restaurants right here within walking distance." Buddy pointed at the seafood restaurant nearby. "If you like fresh seafood, this the best place in town."

"I'm famished," I said. "What about you, Tyler?"

"Sounds good to me!" Tyler agreed.

"It is settled then. If we don't walk over there now, soon we will have to wait in line." Buddy escorted us to the restaurant. It was just starting to get crowded, but we were able to find a table overlooking the marsh and the river.

After placing our order, Buddy pointed out the window, "Do you see where the ramp ends on the dock?" We both nodded. "If you look to the left, do you see the largest mast? That is the Hodos, the catamaran we are sailing to Georgetown."

It clearly was the largest boat on that dock. "It is huge," I said. "What does Hodos mean?"

"It is Greek for 'The Way.' Harvey named it that because he is a Christian and thought it might spark a conversation with people."

Tyler commented, "In John 14:6, Jesus said, 'I am the way, the truth, and the life. No one can come to the Father except though me.'"

I added, "In Acts, the followers of Jesus were called The Way."

"That is very interesting," Buddy remarked.

We finished our dinner, consisting of local shrimp and fish, with sides of slaw and hush puppies. We left the restaurant; and as we turned the corner, I noticed several large wheel barrow-type carts lined up near the walkway to the ramp. Pointing to them, I asked, "What are those used for?"

Buddy replied, "Since it is about a quarter of a mile walk down and back from the boat to the parking lot, the marina supplies these carts. Without them, boaters would wear out walking several times back and forth, toting bags of groceries and supplies."

"Especially in this heat!" added Tyler.

Buddy agreed, "That's why I left a cart here for you to load your stuff." He left us to fetch the cart and followed us to the car.

After loading our duffel bags and groceries, I said, "I didn't know we brought so much stuff. The cart is full!"

We meandered down the sidewalk around the restaurant to the walkway to the docks. The walkway coursed over the marshland. It was low tide, and I could see little crabs scurrying below.

There was an abandoned boat that had obviously been there for years off the left side of the walkway. "What's the deal with that boat?" I asked.

Buddy said, "Boats are abandoned many times – when they sink or when they are damaged from a hurricane. They usually aren't insured, and the owners just leave their boats. They are called derelict boats. You don't even know they are there at high tide."

There was another abandoned sailboat further away on the right side of the walkway. Tyler said, "That sailboat over there looks stripped."

Buddy explained, "After a boat has been left for a period of time, people are free to salvage what they can from the neglected boat."

As we neared the docks, there were two ramps leading to different docks. Both were very steep. I was glad Tyler was in control of the cart. "Why are these ramps so steep?" I asked.

"Low tide," Buddy said. "Their angle changes from steep to level between low and high tide." Buddy motioned to the left ramp, "We take this ramp to the boat."

The base of the ramp brought us to a concrete-floored dock that was not fixed but floated to the level of the tide water. The Hodos was at the end of this dock. "Wow," I exclaimed. "This boat is much bigger than I thought!" True to the pictures that Harvey had shown me, the catamaran was gently floating back and forth – tied to the dock by ropes secured to bollards.

Buddy said to Tyler as he pointed to the rear of the boat, "Leave the cart here." Then Buddy stepped into the back of the boat; and turning to face us, he pointed to a spot in front of him. "When unloading items from the cart, don't try to step onto the boat carrying the stuff. One rock of the boat the wrong way, and you might find yourself in this brackish water! The boat is tied close enough to the dock that you can place the bags or whatever into the cockpit boat." Tyler did as he said and placed the contents of the cart on the ledge.

Then Buddy pointed to a rope that hung down from the edge of the roof of the cockpit. "Grab that rope for stability and climb aboard. Have a seat, and I'll grab some water in the galley and join you." Tyler stepped aboard, and I followed into the cockpit. At first sight, the pictures that Harvey showed me of the Hodos did not compare to the beauty of this vessel!

CHAPTER 3

The Catamaran

The cockpit was the spacious back part of the boat; in boater's terms, it was aft. In the center was a large table – surrounded by vinyl-covered bench seats. To the left or port side, there was a sink and cabinet. Tyler and I sat on the side that faced the inside of the boat. Shortly, Buddy entered with bottled waters, placed them on the table and sat across from us.

"Buddy," I said, "I can't wait to see the rest of the boat! I've never been on a yacht before!"

Buddy replied, "I will be happy to show you around your home for the next few weeks."

After going over a few details of the trip, Buddy said, "Are you ready for the tour?" We both nodded our heads with enthusiasm. "Welcome aboard," Buddy said as he waved his hand in the direction of the entrance to the living quarters.

The salon was comprised of the galley (which was the kitchen), the dining area with a large bench couch on the forward side of the boat and a smaller bench seat on the other side toward the galley. A roomy table was between the bench seats and couch. There were two refrigerators – about half the size of a regular refrigerator, a microwave and coffee maker. To the right of the dining area across from the galley were a helm and a navigation station.

This section had four large windows with bamboo blinds. Below the windows – across the width of the windows – was a fiberglass shelf between the couch and windows. There were two stylish lamps on each side of the bench couch. On either side between the salon and galley were steps. Near the steps on the port side (left side) sat a small flat-screen TV on top of a cabinet.

"This is fabulous," I exclaimed.

Buddy said, "Let me show you the crew quarters." He descended the steps below. Tyler and I eagerly followed. Once in the hallway, I could see two bedrooms, one in aft (back of the boat) and one forward (front of the

Hodos anchored at Cumberland Island, Georgia

boat). Buddy continued, "Aspen, this will be your cabin." He pointed to the aft cabin.

It was a small room – large for a boat though – with a double bed in the center, a shelf on either side and a closet near the door. There was a window on the outer wall that could be opened for ventilation. Interestingly, there was a portal near the bottom of the floor toward the center of the boat. I could clearly see the waterline between the two pontoons of the boat. Pointing to it, I asked Buddy, "Why is this window here?"

Buddy said, "If we have a problem and you are trapped in the cabin, the portal can be broken with a special hammer that is just underneath it and makes for an emergency exit. Each cabin is equipped with this feature. It also makes for a nice view when underway."

Continuing, Buddy said, "Let me show you where the towels and linens are kept." He turned around and walked to the center of the hallway, which had a series of three large cabinets. "This first cabinet has the bed linens; towels are in the middle cabinet; and the third cabinet has toilet paper, paper towels and other supplies and cleaners. If you need something and can't find it, let me know."

Across from the cabinets was the bathroom. "I assume this is our bathroom?" I asked.

Buddy replied, "Yes. It is referred to as a head on a boat."

Tyler was taking it all in. He had not said much but asked, "I see the toilet and the sink. It doesn't have a shower?"

Buddy replied, "It has a shower head, which connects to the sink. The floor has a drain under this floor grate." He pointed to a shower curtain on tracks. "You can shower in here and pull this shower curtain between the sink and toilet."

"Oh, I see," said Tyler.

"This is your cabin, Tyler," Buddy said, pointing to the forward cabin. "It is exactly like Aspen's cabin."

Tyler plopped down on the bed. "Quite nice," he exclaimed.

"Now, if you follow me, I will show you what is called the owner's suite. This will be where Harvey and his wife will live while traveling the islands," Buddy said.

We ascended the small flight of stairs, traversed through the salon and descended another small flight of stairs. The owner's suite was impressive.

There was a couch on one side and a larger flat-screen TV across from it. Next to the couch were a desk and swivel stool. There were shelves and cabinets over the desk and couch. Buddy explained, "This first section is a small living room. To the aft is the master cabin; forward is the master bathroom."

I walked up the hallway. There was a closet on the right and a washer and dryer on the left. "This is amazing," I said, "a washer and dryer on a boat!"

Buddy said, "Yes, that is a very nice feature on this vessel. Oh, and if either one of you would like a real shower, there is one in this bathroom."

I entered the master bathroom. It was as large as our cabins. There was a large shower stall with a sliding door. A teak bench was on one side and teak vertical shelves on the other corner.

"I sure am glad to see this," Tyler said.

"Me, too," I replied.

"There is one more thing I would like to show you," Buddy said. "If you will, follow me to the flybridge."

Buddy led us back up through the salon and out to the cockpit. We climbed up the stairs on the port side. Centered in the middle of the boat was the flybridge. This comprised the ship's wheel and all the gears, pulleys and lines where the sails were adjusted. It had a nice, long bench seat and a Bimini top. The three of us found a place to sit. It was dusk, and the sun was setting in magnificent color. There was a cool breeze. "What do you think?" asked Buddy.

"I think this is the perfect way to end the day," I replied.

Tyler said, "I think I can get used to this."

"Let's get your gear stowed in your cabins, and meet me in the salon for some ice cream," Buddy offered.

We made our way back to the cockpit, gathered up our gear and unpacked in our respective cabins. Once that was completed, we gathered back in the salon where Buddy had several flavors of ice cream and toppings, with bowls and spoons on the table. "This is my weakness," said Buddy. "I have a bowl of ice cream every evening."

We each made our selections and talked about plans for the next day. It had been a long day, and I was ready for bed.

CHAPTER 4

Crewing and Sailing Lessons

I was awakened by the song of the seagulls perched along the bollards of the dock. I pinched myself to make sure this was not a dream. Today Tyler and I were going to learn how to sail the catamaran!

I checked the time on my phone. It was 7:15 a.m. The scent of coffee enticed me to get out of bed. I thought about how hot and humid the day was going to be today, so I selected a light blue tank top and white shorts. After combing my hair, I left my cabin and walked up the stairs to the salon. Tyler and Buddy were sitting at the table, talking over their first cups of coffee. "Good morning," I said.

"Did you sleep well?" Buddy asked.

"Yes. The bed is very comfortable," I replied.

Buddy continued, "Would you like a mug of coffee?"

"Yes, I would, thank you," I answered as I sat down beside Tyler.

Buddy handed me the mug of coffee. Tyler already had placed the half-and-half, natural cane sugar, blueberry bagels and cream cheese that we had brought with us on the table.

"Buddy and I were reviewing our plans for the day," Tyler explained.

Buddy said, "We will take the boat out today and let you both get some hands-on experience with sailing on the ocean. We will be leaving soon after breakfast. It will take us about 30 minutes to reach the ocean."

A little while later, Buddy went topside to the flybridge and started the engines, let them idle and then met us in the cockpit. "Follow me and I will show you how to loosen the lines from the deck cleats."

There were two large, circular fenders hanging from the rail on the deck that protected the sides of the boat from hitting the dock. Close to each one was a large cleat – one on the bow and one on the stern.

"I am going to walk you through what you both are going to do while I am at the flybridge when we get ready to shove off. You see this line is looped through the bottom of the cleat and the other end of the line is wrapped in a figure-of-eight around the cleat on the dock? When I give you the okay, ya'll will step onto the dock, loosen the line about the cleat, place it under the rail onto the deck cleat and return to the boat and return your assigned cleat. Pick up the loose end of the line – called the bitter end. When I give the word, let go of the bitter end, and don't remove the other end of the line that is looped through the cleat. As I maneuver the boat away from the deck, the loose line will slip away from the cleat on the deck, pull it onto the boat and lay it down on the deck. After we leave the dock, remove the fender from the side of the boat by flipping it over the rail; and for now, just leave it on the deck. I will show you how to stow the line and fender once we are out to sea. Aspen, you will be on the bow; and Tyler will be at the stern, releasing us from the dock simultaneously. Any questions?"

I said, "I think I understand."

"I understand as well," replied Tyler.

"Good, I will be moving very slowly; so if you have a problem, let me know."

Buddy returned to the flybridge. Tyler and I were at our assigned spots - ready for Buddy's signal. A few minutes later, Buddy said, "Release the lines now."

I did as I was told, letting the line fall in the water. Once the line was free from the deck cleat, I pulled it from the water and laid it on the deck as Buddy instructed. Then I grabbed the line on the ball fender and pulled it over the rail. I saw that Tyler had finished at about the same time. We both gave Buddy a thumbs-up sign.

Once free from the deck, the boat eased away. Buddy motioned us to the flybridge and said, "Come on up here. There is room for all three of us."

We cautiously walked to the flybridge and sat with Buddy. We were underway but moving slowly as we left the marina because of the "No Wake" signs. The St. Marys River winded through the marshes. We left at high tide to ensure there was enough draft for the boat to miss any sandbars. There was a scattering of what looked like little pots floating in the water. "What are those?" I asked.

"Those are crab pots. As the name implies, people set them in the river to catch crabs. What you see floating is a marker for the crab pot. Boaters must avoid them because the props can get tangled up in the lines between the float and the crab pot. If that happens, the prop cannot turn, and you are dead in the water. I call them mine fields," Buddy responded.

Tyler asked, "What happens when your prop gets tangled in the lines?"

Buddy replied, "Well, the skipper will have to put out an anchor, and he or one of his crew will have to get in the water and free the lines from the prop. If that doesn't work, the skipper has to call for a tow back to the dock and get a professional to release the lines from the prop."

"I guess that would be expensive," Tyler responded.

"Yep," said Buddy. "That's why I try to avoid running over those crab pots." It is nice to have crew to help me keep a lookout."

We made it to the channel that enters the Atlantic Ocean. Clouds started to creep in which generated some wind. Buddy said, "These are good winds for sailing. Ready for your next lesson?"

Buddy pointed to the navy-blue sail bag on the boom. "First, we have to take the sail bag off the mainsail. I have the autopilot on. Aspen, you sit here and keep a lookout. Tyler, you come with me."

Buddy and Tyler removed the sail bag, folded it up and placed it in a compartment on the flybridge. Buddy said, "The next thing we do is raise the mainsail." There was a large net bag full of line under the helm. He took the end of the line out and said, "I am going to wrap the line around this power winch." He placed the handle on top of the winch. "Now I am going to wind the line around this winch. This line raises the mainsail." Tyler and I watched intently. Here was a large button on the deck next to the winch. Buddy applied pressure to it, and the mainsail furled out on the boom.

"Wow, how cool is that?" I exclaimed.

"Once we are underway again, we will trim the sail, adjusting with the wind. We are just about to cross into the Atlantic Ocean. Before we get underway, I'll show you how to stow the lines and fenders. Tyler, it's your turn to keep watch, while I show Aspen what to do."

"Aye, Captain!" said Tyler.

I followed Buddy back to the forward deck. He loosened the line from the cleat and showed me how to neatly loop the line with multiple turns, leaving about half of the line to wrap around the center of the loops tightly about three to four times. Lastly, he took the end of the line, made a small loop, slipped it under the top loops and pulled the bitter end through the smaller loop. There was a vinyl twist lock line holder on the deck rail next to the cleat, and that is where he secured the line.

Next Buddy untied the line from the fender and showed me where to leave the fender on the aft rail. He also showed me how to make two half-hitch knots in the line which make for an easy release.

Buddy said, "When we get back to the dock, first, you will secure the fender on the outside rail, remove the line from the holder, place the loop on the other end of the line through the cleat, toss it around the bollard and make the figure-of-eight loop back on the cleat." Buddy repeated his instruction with Tyler on the aft line and fender.

Buddy and Tyler returned to the flybridge, switching from autopilot to manual control of the engines. We entered the Atlantic Ocean. Buddy turned off the engines and showed us how to control the lines to trim the mainsail. "On either side of the helm, there is a set of rope clutches," Buddy said. "When the handle is down, the clutch holds the line in place and opening the handle releases the line. The blue line controls the mainsail; the red line and black control the jib. Since the winds are light, we will unfurl the jib to catch more wind and increase the speed of the boat."

Tyler and I learned that the jib was on a forward stanchion. There were two sets of lines that went to the jib - one for the starboard side and port side. These lines went from the rope clutches to either side of the boat to the jib, depending on which side of the boat the jib would be un-furled. He released the red line wrapped around the power winch, hit the button, held the black line taut; and the jib automatically unfurled on the port side. Buddy adjusted the lines appropriately. We were officially moving under sail!

Buddy indicated that we were sailing approximately five knots because the winds were light. "Tyler, would you like to take the helm and try your hand at sailing?"

Tyler said, "Certainly, I'll give it a go."

Buddy gave him some instructions about watching the telltales in the jib. When they are losing the wind, the telltales would go slack, and the jib would start luffing. "The jib can be close-hauled or on a reach, depending on the wind," Buddy explained. "Your job, while at the helm, is to steer the boat such that the jib and mainsail are catching the wind."

"My parents have a small sailboat that we sail in the English Channel. My father taught me the basics of sailing," Tyler reminisced. "This is a larger vessel with larger sails."

Buddy replied, "The basics are the same. You are doing a good job keeping on course!"

Tyler managed the helm for a while longer. Buddy announced, "Aspen, it's your turn to take the wheel!"

"I'm not so sure about that! I am not as experienced as Tyler in sailing."

"You won't know until you try, Aspen. I'll be right there with you."

Tyler waited for me to take control of the wheel before he let go. I was apprehensive. I turned the wheel a little too much, and the sails immediately started flapping in the wind.

"Steer a little to the left, Aspen. The wheel is very sensitive and responds to slight turns, not big ones," Buddy explained.

I did the best I could. Tyler was helping adjust the sails. I kept falling off the wind. "I think one of you needs to take the helm," I anxiously said. "I'm a newbie at this."

"Tyler, you can take the helm now. We're going to turn around and go back to the dock now. I'm going to show you how to change tacks," Buddy said. "This will involve both sails. The mainsail will shift as well as we turn to starboard; but don't worry. You will not get hit by the boom if you stay seated." Buddy released the lock on the port side, moved over to the starboard and started pulling in the line through the lock on the starboard side. The jib luffed and moved to the starboard side. The boat barely rocked, but the boom did shift as Buddy said.

As the mainsail sifted, I heard a noise behind me. "What is that noise, Buddy?"

"The boom is secured to what is called a traveler behind you. It doesn't require manual adjustment unless needed in certain weather conditions," Buddy answered. The boat had turned to starboard, and the course was set to return to the entrance of the St. Marys River.

Another thing I learned was that the Intracoastal Waterway and the channels that go to the ocean were marked with navigational aids. They had beacons, so they could be seen at nighttime. Going out to sea, the buoys had green lights on the starboard side and red lights on the port side. Red, right, return was the way to remember the position of the lights. The red lights were on the starboard side when returning from the ocean, and the green lights were on the port side.

When we entered the St. Marys River, Buddy showed us how to furl the jib back on its stanchion and drop the mainsail. After that was done, Buddy started the engines so we could power in. "Aspen, would you take the helm? Just stay in the middle of the channel, watch the buoys and maintain the same speed."

"Sure, I think I can do that," I replied. I grabbed the wheel and kept the boat in the middle of the channel, keeping aware of the channel marker buoys.

After a few minutes, Buddy said, "Aspen, you are doing a great job!"

"Thanks," I replied. "This is much easier than trying to stay on course when sailing."

"It looks like you will make a fine crew - Tyler, the sailor, and Aspen, the power boater!"

Buddy let me power the boat until we approached "No Wake" signs near the marina. "Time for me to take over and dock the vessel. Tyler, you prepare the stern line and fender; Aspen, you prepare the bow line and fender."

"Yes, sir!" Tyler and I said in unison. I reached for the forward fender, tied it to the rail, released the forward deck line and slipped the loop through the cleat; Tyler did the same on the stern.

Buddy said, "Go ahead and put the fenders over the rail" as he neared our spot on the dock. With the aid of the two engines, Buddy masterfully swung the Hodos in its correct position and eased it toward the dock. Buddy gave us the okay when we were close enough to step off the boat safely and finish securing the Hodos to the deck cleats. Once the engines were shut down, we returned to the boat, helped Buddy lower the mainsail and placed it in the sail bag. With everything secured, we decided to walk to town and enjoy a nice lunch at the local Mexican restaurant.

We returned to the boat after lunch. Buddy had plans to take the boat to Cumberland Island tomorrow. He wanted to instruct us about anchoring and using the dinghy. He gave us the rest of the afternoon off.

I asked Tyler, "What do you want to do this afternoon?"

"I would like to walk back into town and visit the St. Marys Submarine Museum," Tyler replied.

"That's a good idea," I replied.

The museum was on St. Marys Street, the main street facing the waterfront. It is the largest museum of its kind in the South. It contains the history of submarines and exhibits. We enjoyed seeing the pictures and models. There was a real, working periscope and a mock-up control room. We learned that in the same county as St. Marys was the submarine naval station that housed the Atlantic Naval fleet of Trident nuclear submarines. Upon leaving the museum, we crossed the street and enjoyed a walk through the park.

We leisurely strolled back to the boat. When we arrived, Buddy was on the bow of the boat, cooking on a portable grill.

"Hi Buddy," I said. "Whatever you are cooking sure smells good!"

"I am grilling steaks and shrimp."

Tyler said, "Could I be of any assistance?"

"Thanks," Buddy replied. "You can check on the corn and potatoes that are cooking in the galley; and Aspen, there are salad fixings in the refrigerator."

"Gotcha," I said. Tyler and I boarded the Hodos, checked on the vegetables and prepared the salad.

Soon after, Buddy came down to the salon with a plate of the steaks and shrimp. "I think it is cool enough outside to eat in the cockpit." He set the plate down and returned to the cockpit to lower the table from the ceiling. The table was set, the meal was set out on the table, and we had a scrumptious dinner. The sun began to set over the marshes. It was a wonderful ending to an exciting day.

CHAPTER 5

Cumberland Island and the Nuclear Submarine

Bright and early the next morning, we set off to Cumberland Island. The mornings were cool until the sun rose. The temperatures could climb to the 90s, and the humidity made it feel even hotter. We made it out of the St. Marys River, still under power, and steered left into the Intracoastal Waterway toward the closest beach on Cumberland Island. It took less than an hour to get to our destination.

As we approached the sandy beach, Buddy said, "We're going to anchor in this area. Then we'll take the dinghy ashore." He put the boat engines in neutral, adding, "Tyler, will you take control of the helm, and I will show Aspen how to lower the anchor."

The anchor - or should I say anchors - were at the tip of the bow. "Which anchor are you going to use?" I asked.

Buddy replied, "Since this is a shallow and sandy bottom, we will use the Danforth fluke anchor." He released the anchor and attached it to the chain that laid in a channel, laying the anchor over the side of the top of the boat. The channel led to a compartment that housed the anchor chain. Buddy opened the compartment and picked up a remote control. "This controls the windlass which lowers and raises the anchor." Buddy pressed the down button, and the anchor and chain dropped into the ocean. "When the anchor hits the bottom, the chain will stop moving."

I looked over the edge of the bow of the boat. The water was clear enough to see the anchor laying in the sand below. The chain was vertical in the water from the boat to the anchor.

"Now Tyler is going to set the anchor." Turning to Tyler, Buddy said, "Tyler, please put the boat in reverse, but do not give it any gas."

Tyler did as Buddy instructed. The boat slowly moved backward. Buddy and I watched the chain as it slowly lengthened and moved to being at an angle to the boat. Then Buddy said to Tyler, "Now put the boat back into neutral." Buddy pulled on the chain, and it was taut. "Okay, Tyler, you can cut the engines now. The anchor seems to be set in the sand sufficiently."

"That did not seem too difficult," I said.

Buddy replied, "Since the water is shallow here and the bottom is sandy, we don't need to put out a lot of chain. The deeper the water and type bottom it is depend on which anchor we use and how much chain. Sometimes it is necessary to put out a stern anchor as well. Catamarans swing differently on an anchor than monohull sailboats."

Next Buddy said, "Let's get ready to go ashore! Be sure and bring a bottle of water, sun lotion and anything else you might need."

I went down to my cabin and changed into a swimsuit, a cover-up and water shoes. I added to my beach bag a towel, some crackers and a plastic grocery bag in case there were any seashells. When I got back to the cockpit, Buddy was showing Tyler the series of ropes and pulleys that lowered the dinghy into the water from the davits. I watched as well. Buddy said it was easier for two people to lower the dinghy because both ends could be lowered at the same time into the water. The stern was heavier because of the outboard motor; and if one person did the lowering, the stern would lower first and then the bow.

Once the dinghy was in the water and tied off to a cleat in the stern, Buddy pointed to a compartment in the cockpit and said, "Aspen, could you get three life jackets, please?"

"Certainly," I replied.

Buddy was already in the dinghy and had pulled it all the way over to the end of the pontoon on the left. I had not noticed until then that there were steps on the end of the pontoons, making it easy to step into the dinghy. Buddy said, "Hand me your beach bag first, and then you can step into the dinghy." I complied. There were two wooden boards that acted as benches, and he motioned for me to sit down. I sat on one side and Tyler on the other side to balance the weight. Buddy sat on the other bench and started up the outboard motor. Then he said to Tyler, "Please untie the line, and we will be on our way."

It did not take us long to get to shore. Buddy cut the engine off and glided in on the beach. "Aspen, you can step off the dinghy now. Tyler and I will pull the dinghy up on the beach a little more, so it won't float away as the tide rises."

As I waited for them to secure the dinghy, I looked around the beach. It was a white sand beach that stretched along the edges of the island. There were no other people around. Buddy said this part of the island was not visited by the tourists who came over on the ferry boat.

We walked a short distance down the beach. Tyler said, "The sand seems to be moving."

I looked, too, stopped walking and put on my water shoes for protection. "What is it?"

Laughing, Buddy said, "It's just a bunch of crabs! They will run from you."

I kept my water shoes on but resumed walking. Sure enough, the crabs scrambled out of our way. A little further down the beach, all sorts of seashells scattered the shoreline. I pulled out my plastic bag and picked up a few different types of shells.

Even though there was a nice breeze, it was starting to get hot. So we turned around and headed back to the dinghy. As we were walking back, two power boats were moving back and forth across the channel. The passengers had on uniforms of some type and carried rifles! "Buddy, are we in any danger? Who are those people?"

Buddy said, "This must be the day a Trident nuclear submarine is going out for maneuvers. These are the military police who patrol the area before the sub leaves the naval station. We will stay put. We can't pull leave now until after the submarine passes by."

Tyler said, "Glad I brought my camera with me. This is a chance of a lifetime!"

"I can take some pictures with my phone as well," I added.

"Well, I guess we can sit in the dinghy and watch the show," replied Buddy.

"Show?" I asked.

Buddy continued, "After the military patrol boats make sure the area is clear, a tugboat leads the submarine through the channel to the ocean. The tugboat sprays water out of the port and starboard sides. It is quite a show."

Not long after that, the tugboat spraying water came into sight. Not far behind came the submarine partially submerged. The patrol boats flanked either side of the submarine at a distance. "I guess the sub is not fully submerged because it is too shallow here."

"That's right," said Buddy "A trench had to be dug from the base to the continental shelf in the Atlantic, so the subs could maneuver through the Cumberland Sound."

We were close enough to the channel to see several men standing atop the submarine. After the sub passed around the tip of the island, Buddy decided that it was safe for us to return to the boat. Once back on board, Buddy said, "I brought some sandwiches and chips for lunch. I thought we could go over to the Cumberland ferry dock. There are some picnic tables there; and after lunch, we could walk to the Dungeness Ruins."

"What a nice surprise!" I exclaimed. "Tyler, I am glad you brought your camera."

Nuclear Submarine leaving Kings Bay, Georgia

"Yes, I fancy this will be a great photo opportunity."

This time I was at the helm, and Buddy instructed Tyler how to raise the anchor. Buddy said, "Aspen, cut the engines on, but keep them in neutral."

"As we pull up the anchor, the boat may move forward some. Don't worry about that. Once the anchor is secured on the deck, put the boat in gear, and steer slowly out into the channel."

I did as I was told. No problems. They made a few adjustments in the anchor's chain and returned to the flybridge, and Buddy took over the helm. It wasn't long before we approached the dock. Tyler and I assumed our positions at the bow and stern; and when Buddy gave the okay, we lowered the fenders and tied the boat off to the dock.

CHAPTER 6

Dungeness Ruins

"Great job!" Buddy said. He went below, gathered the picnic lunch and joined us on the dock; and we walked to shore.

There was a little box with a sign requesting a $5 park entrance fee. Buddy placed the money in one of the envelopes provided. There was a set of picnic tables in a shady area nearby. We selected a spot; and Buddy provided us with a plate of ham and turkey sandwiches, a variety of potato chips and extra bottles of water.

As we were finishing our lunch, Buddy said, "There are many hiking trails on the island. I downloaded a map of the Dungeness Ruins trail. It is about a one-and-a-half-mile hike."

Tyler and I were changing into our walking shoes. Tyler said, "I think we are ready to go."

The trail began with a beautiful walk down a path lined on either side with trees covered in Spanish moss. The path led to a boardwalk that took us to an overlook of beautiful sand dunes with sea oats that was an entrance to a peaceful sandy beach at low tide. "Do we have time to walk on the beach?" I asked Buddy.

"Of course," he replied.

We all took off our shoes and walked to the water's edge. I took a few pictures with my phone. Tyler was photographing as well. We traced our steps back to the boardwalk and put on our shoes. Our next stop was the Dungeness ruins.

The boardwalk crossed over some marshland and ended in a path. The path took us by an old cemetery and then the entrance to the ruins. There were wild turkeys under some trees in the front yard of the estate.

I had picked up an information sheet about the ruins. It had been built by the Carnegie family in the 1880s. The house burned in 1959 and was left in ruins. All that was left were the outer walls of the mansion - a mixture of cut stone and brick. There was a fountain in the front yard that survived the fire. Several horses were in the front yard. They were believed to be descendants from the family polo ponies.

As we continued our walking tour over another boardwalk over the marshes, we saw various wildlife such as a crane flying over the marshland, deer and an armadillo. Several hours after we began our hike, we returned to the dock. "Thank you, Buddy, for taking us here. It was so serene."

"My pleasure," Buddy said. "I like it because it's a national park and protects the wilderness of the island."

Tyler added, "I had a splendid time."

Buddy checked his watch. "We need to get going. It will take us about two hours to get back to St. Marys. We should have plenty of daylight left."

Tyler and I prepared to free the lines, and Buddy climbed aboard. There was practically no wind in Cumberland Sound. We took turns practicing steering the boat under power. As usual, when we neared the marina, Buddy took over and docked the Hodos.

After securing the boat for the evening, I excused myself to shower and wash my hair. Then I went to my cabin to empty my beach bag and tidy up. I moved up to the salon to relax. Buddy appeared from his suite and said to me, "What do you want to do for supper tonight?"

I replied, "I'm pretty tired from hiking. Are there enough leftovers from last night?"

Buddy opened the refrigerator and checked. "I think we can manage another meal from the steaks and vegetables." As Buddy was speaking, Tyler came from his cabin on the way to the shower. "Tyler, are you okay with last night's steak and vegetables for supper tonight?"

"I can't think of anything better," Tyler replied. "I'll be back in a jiffy," he said as he traipsed across the salon and down the steps to the shower.

"I'll help set the table," I said as I got up from the couch.

"Thanks," replied Buddy. "Do you know where everything is?"

"I believe so," I responded. "I'll ask if I can't find everything."

A few minutes later, we sat down for supper. "You know, we have been so busy these past couple of days, I have neglected to say the blessing at our meals," I said. "Buddy, do you mind?"

"No, I don't mind."

I began, "Dear Lord, we thank You for bringing us here safely and for Buddy who has been so gracious to us. We thank You for safe travel to and from Cumberland Island today and its beauty. Thank You for this meal, and thank You for all Your many blessings. In Jesus' Name, Amen."

"Amen!" said Tyler.

Buddy smiled and began eating.

Tyler asked Buddy, "So when are we leaving to deliver the boat?"

"I need to check the weather but probably Tuesday. That will give me today and tomorrow to check the boat's systems and get any more supplies or groceries."

I asked, "Tyler and I would like to attend church somewhere tomorrow. Is that okay with you?"

"I have no problem with that."

I added, "I think the closest church is a Baptist Church in town. We saw a sign for it when we came down on Thursday. We can drive since we still have our rental car. Would you like to come with us?"

"I think I am going to try to catch up on some sleep in the morning. But thanks for asking."

We finished our meal; and as we were cleaning up, Buddy asked, "Do ya'll like to play dominoes?"

"I haven't played in a long time; but, yes, that would be fun," I replied.

Tyler said, "I don't recall ever playing dominoes, but I am willing to learn."

Buddy walked over to a shelf to get a metal tin of dominoes. "I am going to teach you a fun game called chicken tracks." We sat down around the salon table, and Buddy taught us how to play this domino game. We played a couple of times. At the end of the second game, I said, "This was enjoyable, Buddy; but I am getting sleepy. I'm ready to turn in."

We helped put the dominoes back in the tin, and Buddy replaced it on the shelf. "Thank you for your company. I enjoyed playing the game with you both. I think I am ready for bed as well. Good night."

I went to my cabin and went to bed, thinking about what a wonderful day it had been.

CHAPTER 7

The Church Service

On the way to church the next morning, I asked Tyler, "Buddy seems like a nice guy. I wonder why he did not want to go to church with us?"

Tyler replied, "We only met him several days ago. We don't really know him very well."

"Maybe the Lord will provide an opportunity for one or both of us to witness to Buddy while we are transporting the boat," I said.

Shortly afterward, we turned into the driveway of the church. It was an older, brick, two-story structure with the traditional columns at the main entrance to the sanctuary. There was parking on both sides of the church, and we turned in to an open spot. Neither Tyler nor I had packed any fancy clothes. We both wore jeans and polo shirts. As we got out of the car, I was glad to see there were other people dressed casually.

There were several men standing at the steps as we approached the entrance. One older gentleman reached out to shake our hands. "Hello," he said. "My name is Carl."

We shook hands, and Tyler introduced us in reply.

Bob said, "Are you visiting St. Marys?"

I answered, "We are only here for a couple of days. We are crewing on a boat at the marina. We saw your sign when we drove here and wanted to attend church today because we are leaving out on Tuesday."

"We're glad you're here." Carl escorted us inside the sanctuary and guided us to a pew. "I'll pray for a safe journey for you both." We thanked Carl for being so gracious and settled into our seats.

The first 30 minutes of the church service were comprised of lively praise and worship songs. There were three vocalists and five musicians. The announcements followed and then a short time of people fellow-shipping with one another. Several folks exchanged pleasantries with Tyler and me. There was another song while the offering was passed followed by the pastor's message. He spoke from Matthew 28:19-20, where Jesus told His disciples to go to all the nations, baptize people and teach them about Jesus. In closing, the pastor said each person's mission field is unique and revolves around those we associate with in everyday life. The service ended with prayer.

Tyler and I decided to stop for lunch at an Italian restaurant near the waterfront. After we placed our order, I said, "Tyler, I was thinking about the sermon. My parents are Christians; and while growing up, I was surrounded by other Christians. It wasn't until I started college that I realized not everybody receives Christ as their Savior."

Tyler agreed saying, "My parents were Christians, and we faithfully attended church. But after their tragic car crash, as you know, I went to live with my father's brother Allen Dent. He was not a good influence on me. He lived a worldly lifestyle and did not attend church. It wasn't until my freshman year at university that some friends of mine invited me to attend the campus church. That is when I rededicated my life to Christ."

"I think that our mission field will include Buddy and others we may meet in the next few weeks," I said.

Tyler added, "I like the passage in Colossians where Paul tells us that all our work should be done for the Lord and not for men."

About that time, our meal was served. Afterward, Tyler returned thanks to the Lord for our lunch which was delicious. We talked about returning the rental car tomorrow as well as picking up some last-minute items before we left St. Marys on Tuesday.

When we returned to the boat, Buddy was nowhere to be seen. Thankfully, he had given us keys to the entrance to the salon. Upon entering, we noticed various tools lying on the table. "I wonder what's going on?" I queried.

"I don't know," Tyler replied. "I hope I can help out. I'm going to change into some work clothes." Tyler left for his cabin. I had the same idea and went to my cabin to change clothes as well.

While I was still in my cabin, I felt the boat rock, indicating that someone was stepping onto the boat and heard the sliding glass door open. "It's just me," Buddy yelled.

I heard Tyler's voice in the hallway. "What happened?" he asked as he entered the salon. I left my cabin just in time to hear Buddy's reply.

"Just a minor problem. The filter in the desalinization system needed replacement. I had to drive to Jacksonville to purchase a new one."

"What is that?" I asked.

"It turns seawater into fresh drinking water by the process of reverse osmosis."

Tyler asked, "Do you have to store the drinking water?"

"The boat has a 150-gallon water tank. When at sea, the water maker, as I call it, desalinates the seawater into fresh water and stores it in the water tank. Just like in a house, the water is plumbed to the galley and the heads." Buddy pointed to the sink. "In addition, there is that small faucet on the right of the larger sink faucet designated for filling water bottles or whatever."

"Where is this water maker stored?" I queried.

"It's up on the forward deck under that bench seat," Buddy replied. "Tyler, do you want to come help me install the new filter?"

"Certainly," he replied. Tyler and Buddy gathered up the tools and the replacement filter and headed out to the deck. I tagged along as well.

They replaced the filter with no problems. Buddy said, "I'm thirsty. I think it's time to relax in the air conditioning."

I said, "It's so muggy here! The AC is refreshing."

Tyler and Buddy put away the tools, and we settled down in the salon with glasses of iced tea. Buddy said, "It looks like we will be able to leave on Tuesday. The weather looks good for sailing. Tomorrow will be a busy day. I'll go over my checklist in the morning; and after lunch, we can make sure the Hodos is ready to sail."

Tyler said, "We'll drop off our rental car early tomorrow morning. I checked with their website, and someone will drive us back."

"Look at the time," I said. "It's almost 6 o'clock. I feel like having pizza tonight."

"I have an appetite for pizza," responded Tyler.

Buddy said, "There's a great place in town that delivers to the docks. What kind of pizza do ya'll like?"

We decided on one veggie pizza and one meat pizza. In about 30 minutes, the pizzas were delivered to our boat. There were no leftovers! After dinner, we watched a movie. I was in bed by 11 o'clock. I read my devotion and wrote in my prayer journal. I fell asleep while playing a game on my phone.

CHAPTER 8

Preparation Day

Monday morning was our last day before we set sail for the northern Abaco Islands! I gathered my laundry and asked Buddy to instruct me on the use of the washer and dryer. Right after breakfast, Tyler and I stopped off at the grocery store for some last-minute items. We returned the rental car. We did not have to wait long before one of the attendants drove us back to the marina.

While we were walking down the ramp, I said, "Tyler, I am going to miss St. Marys."

"Me, too, except for the bugs and the smell of the marsh."

When we got to the boat, Buddy had not yet returned from town. We put the groceries away. I excused myself and returned to my cabin. Not knowing when I would have Wi-Fi again, I checked my emails and Facebook. I had kept up with Mom or Dad just about every day since we arrived at St. Marys. I figured that I would call now, knowing we would be busy today.

"Hello, Aspen," said Mom. "How are things going?"

"As scheduled, we are leaving early in the morning. We won't have cell reception when we are underway. But I wanted to give you the phone number of the satellite phone in case of an emergency."

Mom replied, "I pray that nothing serious happens."

"I think we will spend some nights at marinas along the Florida coast, and I can check in with you regularly until we cross over to the Bahamas," I explained.

Mom said, "I am so excited for you and Tyler. I hope you have a great time."

"I know we will. Is Dad around?"

"Yes, I'll bring him my phone," replied Mom.

I could hear Mom calling out to Dad. "I'm here, Aspen."

"Hi, Dad. I have a question for you. Do you know anything about the captain, Buddy Sharp?"

Dad responded, "I have met him several times at social functions. He is a long-time friend with Harvey. Why do you ask? Are there any problems?"

"Oh, no! Buddy is a perfect gentleman. He is very friendly and very knowledgeable. He has taught Tyler and me a lot about sailing," I continued. "Tyler and I went to a local church yesterday. We invited Buddy to come with us, but he declined."

Dad said, "Harvey had told me that Buddy had attended church regularly. A few years ago, he left the church and hasn't been back since. Buddy never told Harvey his reason for leaving."

"Thanks for the information, Dad. Please pray for Tyler and me to find a window of opportunity to witness to him." We chit-chatted for a few more minutes. "I'll keep in touch while we are on the Florida coast. When we get to the Abaco Islands, I will email you whenever I have internet reception." We said our good-byes and ended our call.

I left my cabin and found Tyler on his laptop in the salon. "Aspen, I have something to tell you."

"What is it?" I asked

"I just received a text from Hilda, the lady who is taking care of Uncle Allen's home. She got word that he is scheduled to be released from prison in a few days."

"Why?" I asked cautiously.

"She indicated that he was released for good behavior, but he will be on parole. He can't leave England."

"I don't suppose it is going to be a problem then," I replied.

"I hope not," Tyler answered. "I told her not to let him know of my awareness that he has been released."

I asked, "Does she know you are leaving tomorrow?"

"No. She thinks I am in Atlanta."

"Does Allen know your cell phone number or email address?" I asked.

Tyler answered, "No. I changed my contact information when I moved to Georgia."

"Do you trust Hilda not to say anything?"

"Absolutely," Tyler said. "She is my mother's cousin. I hired her to take care of Uncle Allen's house. She holds no loyalty to him."

"That's a relief," I said. "Is Buddy here?"

"No. He texted me that he would be here around noon."

I checked my watch. "Good. We have a little time to talk about him." I told him about my conversation with my dad. "I hope we can find an opportunity to talk to Buddy."

Tyler agreed, "Though he is quite friendly and considerate, I think he is carrying some baggage from his past."

I said, "I think we can find opportunities to share with him ways that God has blessed us."

"Indeed," Tyler replied.

Buddy returned to the boat a short time later. "Hello," he said. "I think I have all the items I need for emergency repairs."

"I hope we don't encounter any problems," I responded.

"True," he replied. "Experience has taught me it is better to be prepared before you leave the dock."

Buddy stowed his supplies. As planned, after lunch, we met in the cockpit and went over the pre-cruise checklist. Buddy explained, "I oversee the engine, generator, fuel and water tanks. The lifejackets are in this compartment under the bench seat in the center. Each one has a number. Mine is 1; Tyler, yours is 2; and Aspen, yours is 3. He raised the lid and said, "I want you to find your respective life jacket and adjust the straps to fit."

"I have never seen a life jacket like this," I said.

Buddy explained, "They are inflatable life vests. They are lightweight; but if you go overboard, there is a carbon dioxide cylinder that - either manually or automatically - will inflate for maximum buoyancy."

The gray life vests were identical, but each one had a different color seam. Mine was red, Tyler's was blue, and Buddy's was yellow. Each life-jacket was equipped with a whistle and reflector strips. "This is not what I expected," I said.

Buddy pointed to another set of life jackets on the other side of the compartment. "These are your more conventional life jackets. When we are underway and are topside, we will wear these. In case of inclement weather, we will wear the life vests. There are a few more safety items," Buddy continued. He opened a bag and handed us what looked like a watch. "These are overboard alarms. You can either wear it on your wrist or ankle in normal sailing conditions. In bad weather, you can attach it to your life vest or wear it."

Tyler asked, "If we fall overboard for any reason, this will automatically send a signal?"

"Correct," Buddy replied. "In simple terms, it is activated when you enter the water. Then an alarm sounds on my navigation equipment with your GPS coordinates."

"Why does this life jacket have a hook?" I asked.

"If we are in a storm and we need to be on deck for any reason, there is a length of line on either side of the boat. You can tether your vest to the line as a further safety measure to prevent falling overboard."

"I pray we don't get into a storm, but I'm thankful you are so prepared," I added.

Buddy nodded, "I feel that way as well. We need to go over some more items on my checklist."

We headed up to the deck. Buddy briefed us on the sails and hardware, including the mast and halyards, the mainsail and reefing. We already had been trained on the winches, ropes and fenders.

Buddy continued his checklist. "Once underway, all of us will keep a lookout. It is my job to maintain the ship's log and charting plots. Tomorrow I will teach you how to use the chart plotter and radar on the Raymarine navigation system."

Tyler said, "This is so exciting!"

"Now there are a few other minor things. Aspen, how do you feel about being in charge of preparing our meals while we are at sea?"

I replied, "I will be happy to."

We spent the rest of the afternoon swabbing down the decks, cleaning the windows and tidying up the living quarters. After we had completed our tasks, Buddy took us out for dinner.

During dinner, Buddy said, "We will leave at first light in the morning. Sunrise is about 6:30 a.m. Set your alarms for 5:30 in the morning."

"I guess we should get ready for bed when we get back to the boat," I said.

"Absolutely," Buddy replied.

Tyler asked, "Will we have time for breakfast?"

"I'll have the items ready. Aspen will prepare breakfast after we are underway," Buddy answered.

We returned to the catamaran around 8 p.m. I was in bed about 30 minutes later. I knew it was going to be hard to fall asleep so early. During my devotion and prayer time, I asked the Lord to calm me down, so I could relax and go to sleep. The next thing I knew, I woke up to my 5:30 a.m. alarm on Tuesday morning and jumped out of bed wide awake.

CHAPTER 9

St. Augustine, Florida

I changed into comfortable clothes and ran up the stairs to the salon. Buddy was brewing the coffee. "Hi Buddy," I said.

"Good morning," he replied. "I see you had no trouble waking up this morning."

About that time, Tyler wandered in yawning, "Good morning as well. I will be fully awake with my first cup of coffee."

We sat down, and Buddy briefly went over this morning's schedule. "As soon as I get the engines warmed up, Tyler, you can disconnect the shore power and stow the power cord. Aspen, you make sure all the hatches are batten down. Then we will be ready to release the lines."

Things went smoothly. As we left the dock, Tyler and I stowed the lines and fenders and met Buddy on the flybridge. We were underway! Buddy said, "Since we will be moving slowly until we get to the main channel, now would be a good time to fix us some breakfast."

Happy that I had an important job, I made my way back to the galley. Buddy had stocked the galley with a variety of choices. I chose bacon, scrambled eggs and toast. Fortunately, none of us were picky eaters. I sat the plates on a tray and cautiously traversed the steps to the flybridge. "A little help here?" I asked.

Tyler grasped the tray and set it on the bench seat. He gave a plate to Buddy. "Before I settle down, would anyone need another cup of coffee?"

"Yes, please," said Buddy, passing his mug to Tyler, who handed me both mugs.

"I'll be right back." The coffee mugs for sailing were insulated with tops to avoid spillage. I returned with the refills and handed them to Tyler. "Buddy, do you mind if I eat my breakfast down below?"

"Not a problem. We will be moving slowly for a while," he replied.

I returned to the salon, got my plate and coffee and returned to the cockpit. The sun was starting to rise, casting a colorful glow into the sky. I prayed that our journey would be safe.

By the time I finished cleaning up after breakfast, we were in the main channel that led to the Atlantic Ocean. I climbed back up to the flybridge on the starboard side of the boat. Buddy was in the center at the helm. Tyler sat beside him on the port side.

Buddy said, "As soon as we pass through these jetties, we will put up the sails."

"How far will we travel today?" I asked.

"My plan is to make it to St. Augustine. The weather looks good today, and the seas are smooth."

Tyler asked, "How long will it take us to get there?"

"About twelve hours," Buddy replied. "If the winds die down, we can always power in."

As we entered the Atlantic Ocean, there were several shrimp boats casting their nets. Each boat had a cloud of seagulls following in their wake. "How far offshore are we, Buddy?" I asked.

"About a mile," he replied, "There is a lot of shallow water near the beaches."

As we traveled down the Florida coast, Buddy kept us informed about where we were relative to the shore. We passed Fernandina, Amelia Island and Jacksonville. The weather could not have been better. Tyler and I took turns at the helm. Buddy instructed us how to follow our course on the chart plotter. He also showed us how to use the autopilot. Whenever we had a straight course, we set the degree that we were traveling, and the autopilot kept us on track.

Around 5 p.m., Buddy said, "We're approaching the entrance to the Matanzas River. Let's go ahead and lower the mainsail now."

We brought in the jib earlier. Tyler and I assisted Buddy with the mainsail. Buddy switched to engine power. "The entrance is narrow for our size boat, so maneuvering is a little tricky. Get the boat hooks out in case the current moves us close to the pylons."

I stood watch on the starboard side, and Tyler was on the port. Fortunately, we were approaching at high tide. Our draft was four feet. We did not have to worry about hitting bottom because the width of the catamaran was the difficulty. Buddy did a perfect job steering the boat through the entrance to the river. Once through, the river widened into a bay.

Up ahead was the drawbridge. Previously, Buddy had put me in charge of the Intracoastal Waterway book that had listings of drawbridges and marinas. Our boat's mast was 74 feet tall, making it too tall to go under most fixed bridges on the ICW. Usually, we could only go through drawbridges. The ICW book gave the times that the drawbridges opened. The one at St. Augustine opened at 6 p.m. By the time we got to the bridge, we only had to wait a few minutes.

Once passing through the drawbridge, Buddy explained, "St. Augustine has moorings instead of marinas for transient boaters. When we approach an empty mooring, Tyler, I want you to take the boat hook and go to the bow of the boat. I will be idling in very slowly. Once I select the location, you will see a large floating ball with a shackle and a length of wire with an eyelet. Aspen, I want you to take two lines from the dock box and secure one end to each of the forward cleats. When you can reach the eyelet with the boat hook, give me a thumbs up and I will put the boat in neutral. Then Aspen, you should be able to take one of the lines, slip it through the eyelet, bring it back to the cleat and secure it. Do the same thing on the other side. Once secured, Tyler, you can release the boat hook."

Drawbridge at St. Augustine, Florida

At the appropriate time, Buddy idled slowly to the selected mooring. Tyler retrieved the eyelet; and as fast as I could, I gave Buddy the thumbs up. Buddy turned off the engines. I threaded the two lines through the eyelet and secured them back to the cleat.

Buddy came down to the bow. "Good job, crew! All I have to do is adjust the length of the two lines to allow for the tide." He continued, "Catamarans swing differently than monohulls on a mooring."

"How do you pay for the mooring?" I asked.

"The dockmaster will come by in a dinghy and collect our money for the night's stay," Buddy answered. "We got here early enough to take the dinghy into town and have dinner. I know a nice Cuban restaurant near the dinghy dock."

Tyler added, "I haven't experienced Cuban cuisine before."

"I think you both will enjoy it," Buddy said. "As soon as we freshen up, we will go ashore.

We returned to the boat after dinner. It had been a long day, and none of us felt like walking around. Buddy checked the weather. The forecast called for rain and possible thunderstorms tonight and in the morning. Buddy said, "I think we can sleep in tomorrow morning. I'll check the weather again when I wake up."

"I'd rather stay here in the rain than sail in it," I said.

It was only 10 p.m., but we all decided to turn in. I fell asleep as it started to rain.

CHAPTER 10

Cape Canaveral

I t was still raining when we awoke on Wednesday morning. After breakfast, Buddy was reviewing the nautical charts.

"Where is our next stop?" I asked.

"It depends on the weather and sea conditions," Buddy replied. "Because of the fixed bridges, we will have to sail around Cape Canaveral, keeping at least a mile offshore."

Tyler asked, "What is the nearest place that has a marina we can reach?"

Buddy said, "Ft. Pierce is about a 10-hour trip from here."

I said, "That is not as far as we traveled today."

"No, it is not - if we don't run into any rough seas or weather, which will slow us down," Buddy replied.

Since the internet was available at the mooring, I checked my email and social media. I checked in with my mom and gave her an update.

Buddy said, "I guess we can head out now so that we should be able to arrive at Ft. Pierce around 9 or 10 o'clock tonight. Aspen, go ahead and call the city marina and book us a dock."

Soon after that, we unhooked from the mooring and idled through the pass that set our path out to the Atlantic Ocean. The day started out well. It was a sunny day with fair wind.

Buddy said, "We are starting to get some wind from the south, and it will hit us head on."

"What does that mean?" I asked.

"It means that if the waves increase, they will hit the boat at the bow and we may get tossed about a bit."

Tyler asked, "Do you think we should put on our life jackets?"

"You can put on the regular jackets if you wish. I don't think we need to worry about the inflatable life vests right now," Buddy said.

Just as a precaution, I retrieved all three life jackets and placed them at the helm.

Things seemed to be going well until about 7 o'clock. The winds picked up, and the waves got bigger. Buddy said, "I am going to power. Let's drop the sails."

By that time, we all were wearing our life jackets. Tyler and I lowered the mainsail. We had not been using the jib. We stowed everything we could.

Buddy said, "It is getting dark way too soon. I am afraid we are heading straight into a storm. Aspen, you better get the life inflatable life vests. "

My heart was racing. I tried to calm myself. "It is a storm, not a hurricane," talking to myself. I reached for the life vests. Buddy already had attached the overboard alarms. I put mine on and brought the other ones to Tyler and Buddy. I did not see another boat in sight.

I returned to the flybridge and heard Tyler ask, "Is that a space shuttle?"

Buddy replied, "Yes, we are going to round Cape Canaveral."

"The shuttle is lit up like a lighthouse!" I exclaimed.

Buddy said, "It's a good thing with the sky so dark."

I said, "The boat is really rocking."

Buddy explained, "The wind has picked up to 20 knots, and the waves are swelling at six feet."

Tyler was on lookout. Suddenly, he spoke up, "Look, there is a bright light in front of us!"

Buddy said, "I'll check the AIS for any other identifiable vessels. I don't see anything on the monitor. Maybe it is a fixed light, but I will follow its course. It is going south as well."

"What does AIS mean?" Tyler inquired.

"AIS is an acronym for automatic identification system. This means that vessels in our immediate area with AIS are automatically traced, so we know their location relative to our vessel. It is invaluable in times like this," Buddy explained.

"Do you mind if I go below?" I asked.

"Of course not, Aspen. Go right ahead. Tyler and I can take care of things."

I was so relieved. I kept my life vest on and sat in the cockpit - just in case they needed something. It was a good thing that I did not get seasick. The boat was like a roller coaster; the waves were crashing through the boat's trampoline netting. I tried to relax but couldn't. A little while later, it started raining. I felt the boat lower in speed. Tyler later told me we were moving about 2 to 5 knots through the storm.

I looked out from the back of the boat. A white bird of some sort was following the boat. Why was a lone seagull out in this storm following the boat? I felt peace. Maybe God had put the bird there to follow us. Then I thought about the guiding light in the distance. I couldn't help but think it was another marker from God. I truly believed that God protected us and kept us safe through the storm.

The wind finally died down, and the swells were not as bad. I decided to go back up to the flybridge. "How is it going guys?" I queried.

Buddy replied, "I think the worst is over. The cloud cover is breaking up, and the sky is getting lighter. We just must get through these shipping lanes, and the next stop is Fort Pierce."

"Thank the Lord!" I exclaimed.

"Amen to that," returned Tyler.

CHAPTER 11

Fort Pierce, Florida

It was twilight as we went through the Fort Pierce South Gate Draw Bridge. Fortunately, the City Marina was just inside the bridge. Buddy called the dockmaster about our approach, and several staff members assisted us in docking the Hodos. We were all exhausted; and after a quick dinner of sandwiches, we all went to bed.

I awoke Thursday morning refreshed. After my prayers and devotional, I went to the galley to make coffee and breakfast. Shortly after, Buddy entered from his side of the boat. "Good morning, Aspen," he said. "I'm ready for a mug of coffee."

I poured him a mug full, handed it to him and said, "It sure is a good morning!"

Buddy turned to sit at the table, and I served him grits and bacon. "Boy, am I hungry!"

Soon after, Tyler came to the salon, and we all sat down to talk about our next leg of the journey. Buddy reviewed the navigational chart and said, "Our next stop will be Lake Worth."

"Isn't that near West Palm Beach?" I asked.

"Yes," Buddy replied.

"I have a friend who lives there."

Buddy said, "We will have to wait for a window to cross the Atlantic. Depending on the weather, we may be docked several days. Maybe you will have time to meet up with her."

I answered, "That would be nice."

"After we fill up the fuel and water tanks, we will head out for Lake Worth."

We left the inlet and set out to sea. Tyler was at the helm. Buddy asked him to give an update on the sea and weather conditions.

After reviewing the various gauges and the chart plotter, Tyler said, "We have northeasterly winds, a following sea and the winds varying from nine to 22 knots. The seas are three to six feet."

"How long should it take us to get to Lake Worth?" Buddy asked.

"Let's see. It is about 53 nautical miles. With the wind creating a following sea and under power, I would say about four hours."

Buddy responded, "Your calculations seem correct."

"Impressive!" I responded.

Buddy added, "Tyler, you take the helm for the first two hours; and then Aspen will take the second two hours."

CHAPTER 12

Lake Worth, Florida

The conditions were near perfect. I manned the helm at that time. We were under power and had the jib furled. We were not more than a mile offshore, and I had to change course several times to dodge fishing boats.

As we approached the Lake Worth inlet, it was apparent that a freighter was following us, so Buddy took over the helm. We docked at the Municipal Marina at 1 p.m. Once settled, Buddy checked the weather forecast, and the next few days called for scattered rain and windy conditions. "It looks like we will have to wait a few days for our window to cross over to West Bank," Buddy reported to us. He added, "Aspen, you will have a little time for see your friend now."

"Thanks for the info. I'll give her a call." Back in my cabin, I searched Robin's number in my contacts. Robin answered in a few rings. Having me listed in her contacts as well, she said, "Hello stranger, what a blast from the past!"

"Hi Robin. I am in Lake Worth for a day or two and thought we might catch up if you are free."

"Sure. Where are you staying?"

I replied, "Well actually, I am crewing on a catamaran, and we are docked at the Municipal Marina."

"I don't have to work tomorrow, and I am familiar with the marina. Why don't I pick you up in the morning about 10 o'clock? I can show you some of the sites and then eat lunch."

"Sounds great. Oh, and can I bring Tyler along?"

"If I remember, is that the fellow you met in England?"

"Yep," I replied.

"Sure. I can't wait to meet him! See you in the morning!"

I went up to the salon and sat down with Tyler, who was checking his email. He had a grim look on his face.

"What's the matter, Tyler?"

Lake Worth seen from Peanut Island, Florida

"Hilda sent a distressing email. The message read, 'Allen returned to home yesterday. He asked me why I was in his house. I told him I was there, as usual, dusting and vacuuming. He asked me who was paying me, and I told him. Allen told me to leave and not to come back. I told him that he better behave, or I would find out who his parole officer was and call him. Allen literally shoved me out the door.'"

"That's not good," I commented.

"I replied to her email and advised her to keep me updated," Tyler said.

"Changing the subject, do you want to come with me and Robin tomorrow?"

"Yes, that will take my mind off of Uncle Allen," Tyler replied. "Remind me how you know her?"

"When I was a freshman at Emory, I met Robin at church. We had a lot in common and became friends. After she graduated, she returned to her home here in West Palm Beach, where she is a manager in her parents' retail business."

Tyler asked me, "Do you want to take a walk and look around?"

"Sure. Let me get my walking shoes, and I'll be ready."

As we stepped off the boat onto the dock, I thought I saw movement in the water. "Tyler, do see anything moving in the water?"

We looked between the dock and the boat, peering into the water. Tyler pointed to something swimming in the water. "Look," he exclaimed. "There was a large fish or animal swimming around the boat!"

I looked closer where he was pointing. "I think that's a manatee," I replied. "I've seen them on documentaries, but this is the first time I have actually seen one. They are also called sea cows."

Tyler added, "They must travel in groups" and pointed around the corner of the dock. "There are several more swimming around."

We were still close to the boat; so I walked over to the cockpit, noticed the sliding door was ajar and said, "Buddy, are you close by?"

"Yes, I'm in the salon."

"There are some manatees out here; I thought you might like to see them."

He replied, "I'll be right out."

Momentarily, Buddy departed from the boat to view the gentle giants.

Buddy said, "I never tire of looking at these magnificent animals. Thanks for letting me know, Aspen."

CHAPTER 13

Peanut Island and West Palm Beach, Florida

After the aggregation of manatees moved on, I asked Buddy, "Have you ever been here before?"

"A few times," he replied. "Peanut Island is just across the inlet and is accessible by our dinghy. Would you like to go there?"

"That sounds wonderful," I said.

"Tyler, will you help me get the dinghy lowered into the water?"

"Certainly," Tyler responded.

"I will grab some bottled waters," I said.

It didn't take any time to cross the inlet to Peanut Island. We tied our dinghy off at the guest dock.

As we left the dock, Buddy said, "Peanut Island got its name from shipping peanut oil back in the 40s. It has been renovated, and now there is a nice walking path around the island. We are not far from the start of the path and can take a walk around the island."

On the path, we saw some unusual trees. There was a plaque that described them. They were called gumbo limbo trees and had a red, peeling bark. Also on the path was a bomb shelter built in the 1960s for President Kennedy. Also along the path was a former Coast Guard Station, which is now a maritime museum. The final point of interest along the path was a boardwalk through the mangroves.

Before leaving Peanut Island, we stopped at the picnic area and I passed out the water bottles. Sitting nearby was an older couple. They greeted us as we walked by. "Would you like to sit with us?" the lady asked.

"Why thank you," I said. I sat across from them, and Tyler and Buddy followed my lead.

"Are you tourists?"

"Not really," I answered, "We are at the marina over there (pointing to our boat), just passing through."

The lady responded, "Where is your next destination?"

Buddy responded, "The West End in the Northern Bahamas."

"Are you on vacation here?" I asked.

"No, we live here," the lady replied. "I left Iran back in the 1970s. I had some Muslim friends here. Then I met William (pointing to her husband) one day, who was a Christian. We became friends. After many long chats about the differences in our religious beliefs, he led me to the Lord Jesus and I converted to Christianity. Soon after that, we were married."

"That is wonderful!" I exclaimed. "My name is Aspen, and this is my friend Tyler. We are Christians as well!"

The lady smiled and said, "My name is Amaya."

"So nice to meet you and your husband," Tyler said.

William said to Buddy, "I am William and your name, sir?"

"Buddy," and they shook hands.

"Are you a Christian?"

Buddy hesitated and said, "Well, I guess you could call me a silent Christian."

William did not press any further and said, "May we pray for you and your friends for safe travel?" They bowed their heads as did we.

"Dear Lord, we pray for our newfound friends in Christ. We pray for safe passage across the ocean to the Bahamas and beyond. Thank You for all Your blessings upon us. In Jesus' Name, Amen."

"Thank you for your prayers," I said. "It was a pleasure meeting you both."

We waved one, last goodbye and walked back to the dinghy. "This was just lovely, Buddy. Thanks for bringing us here."

"I am so glad we met up with that caring couple," Tyler said.

"I thought you would like it. Peanut Island is a popular place on the weekends for boaters and family gatherings. It isn't crowded during the week."

On the ride back to the boat, Buddy seemed pensive and didn't say much until we reached the dock. By the time we returned to the Hodos, it was time for dinner. Buddy took us to a restaurant within walking distance that had outdoor seating. We enjoyed a platter of hamburgers and French fries.

Toward the end of our meal, I said to Buddy, "Tyler and I are here for you - if you ever need to talk about anything."

Buddy replied, "Thank you. I'll keep that in mind."

We made it safely back to the boat before dark. After a rousing game of dominoes, it was time for bed. I was excited about meeting with Robin on Friday.

True to her word, Robin met Tyler and me at the pier at 10 o'clock. She gave us a tour of Palm Beach and West Palm Beach. We drove through glitzy neighborhoods and the main street filled with boutiques, art galleries and museums. Even though Lake Worth and Riviera Beach were in the same county, they were as different as day and night. Palm Beach and West Palm Beach were two of the most affluent areas in Florida whereas Lake Worth and Riviera Beach were much poorer areas. After a fabulous lunch at a local Mexican restaurant, she dropped us back off at the marina.

We returned to the boat, where Buddy was studying the current weather conditions. "It looks like we are good to leave early in the morning. The weather conditions look good for a crossover to West End."

"Is there anything we need to do in preparation?" I asked.

"You and Tyler can fill up the gas and water tanks. I'm going to take a little dive and check out the propeller and speed indicator."

"Why is that?" Tyler asked.

"I want to remove any barnacles to ensure the best conditions for crossing the Atlantic tomorrow," Buddy replied. "Oh, and we need to get to bed early because I want to leave before sunrise before the cargo ships leave in the morning. I don't want to follow a freighter out as we leave that narrow inlet."

"For what time should we set our alarm clocks?" I asked.

Buddy said, "4 a.m."

CHAPTER 14

West End, Grand Bahamas

On Saturday morning, I jumped out of bed when the alarm on my phone chimed at 4 a.m. Buddy and Tyler were milling around by the time I stepped up to the salon. Three coffee mugs were already on the table. We said our "good mornings" as Buddy motioned for us to sit down.

"Let's go over our plans," Buddy said. "Aspen, you and Tyler secure the cabin; and I will start the engines. Once free from the dock, we will idle out through the inlet. Hopefully, we will make it to open water before the tankers shove off this morning."

Tyler and I made sure the hatches were closed, with drawers, cabinets and any loose items stowed.

When Buddy was ready to leave, he called us to release the boat from the dock. After stowing the fenders and lines, we were underway. The Hodos glided silently through the water toward the mouth of the inlet. Along with our navigation lights and the lights from the city, Buddy only had to use the search light once to illuminate a navigational buoy marker to ensure he was entering the channel that led to the ocean.

It was twilight when we entered the Atlantic Ocean. We were still under power. Buddy set the autopilot once we were in open water. "Aspen, will you prepare some breakfast for us?" Buddy asked.

"Certainly," I replied. "I'll let you know when it is ready."

I left the flybridge and moved to the salon. I prepared scrambled eggs, toast, slices of cantaloupe and, of course, more coffee. I let the guys know breakfast was ready, and they came down shortly thereafter.

Buddy kept watch at the navigation station, while Tyler and I sat facing the front windows and enjoyed a fabulous sunrise.

"How far is it to West End, Buddy?"

Buddy replied, "About 60 miles."

Tyler added, "How long will it take for us to get there?"

Buddy replied, "According to my calculations, now that we are in the Gulf Stream - with current wind and sea conditions - we should be there in about four to five hours under power."

"Will we put up the sails?" I inquired.

"No, it is better to stay under power when crossing the Gulf Stream because we can stay on course more accurately," Buddy continued. "There are a few things we should have ready when we get to the breakwaters at West End." Buddy reached into a drawer and pulled out a yellow, square flag. "We will need to secure this quarantine flag to our port outrigger. We can take it down as soon as we pass customs. Also, have your passports available."

Noting that I lost cell reception once we left the coast of Florida, I asked, "Will we have cell reception in the Bahamas?"

"Only if you got a SIM card for your cell phone," Buddy replied.

"Yes, I have a SIM card. I had to get one when we went to England."

Buddy continued, "I have a satellite phone for any emergencies."

We chatted a little more. Tyler helped me clean up, while Buddy returned to the flybridge.

"We will join you in a few," Tyler said to Buddy.

We sailed across the Gulf Stream with no problem. There was little boating traffic for a Saturday. We saw one tanker and a few boaters.

We made it to West End, Grand Bahamas, about 11 a.m.. Tyler hoisted the quarantine flag as we entered the breakwaters.

We found a spot on their spacious dock at the marina at West End. The gas attendant pointed us to the yellow Customs building next to the entrance of the marina.

Buddy secured his Coast Guard documentation of the vessel, the Customs paperwork; and we all had our passports as we left the dock and walked a short distance to the building. Because our boat was over 35 feet long, it cost $300. The Customs agent said it was good for a year if we stayed in the Bahamas; but if we left and returned in more than 90 days, we would have to pay another $300.

CHAPTER 15

Great Sail Cay

Buddy decided to anchor just outside the marina. To our surprise, we were close enough to get the Wi-Fi from the marina. The water in the Bahamas is shallow in many areas. It is clear and blue and easy to see to the bottom. We enjoyed leisure time and soaking up some sun.

There was no daylight savings time in the Bahamas, so we lost an hour. I went to bed at 7:30 p.m. (8:30 p.m. back home). I woke up at 5 a.m. Sunday and couldn't go back to sleep. I decided to get in some internet time. Tyler and Buddy joined me in the salon about an hour later.

During breakfast, Buddy said, "Our next leg of the trip is to Great Sail Cay."

"How long will it take to get there?" I asked.

"About nine hours - give or take," Buddy replied. "As soon as we finish breakfast, we'll head out. There's really not much to do there. It's uninhabited, but there is a well-sheltered cove."

After we were underway, Buddy told me to take the lookout as we took a cut through the west bank in Goodwill Channel. The channel was very shallow. I could easily see the bottom. In fact, the water was so clear that I could easily see the starfish below. "How deep are we, Buddy?"

"The channel averages about 10 feet in depth, but we have to watch out for shallow sand banks," Buddy replied.

The weather was beautiful. We didn't see another boat while crossing the channel.

We arrived at Great Sail Cay about 4 p.m. Buddy anchored in a region near mangrove trees.

Tyler and I were admiring the scenery. Buddy said, "I'm sure you have seen that glass-bottom kayak affixed to the side of the boat. Why don't you and Tyler use the kayak and row around the area?"

"Are you sure Harvey won't mind?" I asked.

"Of course not," Buddy replied. "If he were here, he would want you to have a little fun."

With help from Buddy, we lowered the kayak into the water of the aft of the boat, got out life jackets and went for a ride.

"I must say there is not much to see on the bottom here," Tyler commented.

"I agree, but it is fun. There is not much current and no wind."

There was another sailboat nearby. "Let's go say hello," Tyler said.

We paddled our way to the monohull sailboat. There was a couple sitting out on the bow. We pulled alongside and talked for a while. It turned out they were from Yorkshire, England. My parents and I visited Yorkshire while we were in England. Tyler enjoyed talking with the Brits.

We said our goodbyes and headed back to the Hodos. Buddy helped us aboard and secured the kayak.

After showering, we enjoyed hamburgers and hot dogs on the "Lido Deck" of the boat. Obviously, there was no internet; so we played a game of dominoes before going to bed. I fell asleep about 8:30 p.m. It had been another long day.

CHAPTER 16

Shallow Water

On Monday morning, Buddy had a frustrated look while sitting at the navigation station when I came up for breakfast. "What's up, Buddy?" I asked.

"I'm having trouble getting a weather frequency on the side band radio. It's frustrating not having Wi-Fi reception to check my NOAA weather app."

Tyler was sipping a cup of coffee and asked, "Mind if I give it a go, Buddy?"

"Sure, have at it!" Buddy replied as he relinquished his seat for Tyler.

Tyler adjusted the knob, looking for any frequency. "I hear a faint signal." He turned up the volume some; and though there was static, he found a station with NOAA weather for the area.

Buddy listened to the forecast. "Sounds like we'll be going through choppy seas and wind at 20 knots with gusts."

"That doesn't sound good," I said.

"It will probably take us a little longer to get to our next mooring at Crab Cay, but hopefully we will catch some breaks in the weather."

We pulled up anchor about 10 a.m. As soon as we left the sheltered side of Great Sail Cay, the winds started blowing, causing three- to five-foot seas. The boat was swaying back and forth as we journeyed to our next destination. I was not used to this; and per Buddy's suggestion, I stayed below decks most of the day.

The winds were still bad when we arrived at Crab Cay, another uninhabited island. Tyler and Buddy managed to set the anchor in a protected cove. There were a few other sailboats already anchored there.

During supper, we felt a thump. "What is that?" I asked nervously.

"Sounds like we have hit bottom," Buddy said as he rose from his chair and walked out to the cockpit. After surveying the situation, he added, "The tide is going out. We need to reset the anchor farther out."

"How are we going to do that?' Tyler asked.

"We can't move by starting the engines because we are in too shallow of water," Buddy explained. "One of us will have to swim down to the anchor and drag it further out until the boat is out of danger of hitting bottom again. Then we will use the winch to secure the anchor."

Tyler said, "Obviously, we are in shallow water. I'll volunteer."

Buddy said, "We are in less than four feet of water. After you reach the anchor, you can probably stand up and drag it by grabbing the chain and swim it out a few feet. You won't need to go far before I can safely start the engines and get to deeper water."

"Sounds like a plan," Tyler said. "I'll go change into my swim trunks and get my life jacket and mask."

Buddy and I went to the bow and watched Tyler free up the anchor. He walked it out a few feet until he had to tread water. Buddy checked the depth finder and said to Tyler, "The depth finder is showing six feet of water. Can you swim the anchor out a few more feet?"

Tyler gave us a thumbs up, holding the chain and dragging the anchor out farther away from the shore. Five minutes lapsed, and Tyler popped his head out the water. Buddy checked, and we were in 10 feet of water. Buddy yelled, "That's good. Drop the anchor chain, and swim back now." A few minutes later, Tyler was at the stern ladder. I gave him a beach towel as he climbed back into the cockpit.

Buddy was at the top helm. "Thanks, Tyler. You did a great job! Aspen, please go to the bow and be ready to use the winch; and I'll start the engines."

Buddy let the engines idle, and the boat slowly moved forward. When the boat was safe from hitting bottom again, he said, "Aspen, pull in the anchor chain until you can see the anchor at the bottom and give me a thumbs up." I signaled to him when I completed my task, and Buddy cut the engines.

"I think we'll be set for the night," Buddy said. "We work well as a team!"

The boat rocked and rolled all night, but the anchor held.

CHAPTER 17

Crab Cay

It turned out we had to stay anchored at Crab Cay for another day. On Tuesday, the winds continued to blow, and we had some rain as well. We all got to sleep in a little later that morning. It was nice taking a break from sailing for a day. By evening, the winds had calmed, and the rain had stopped. The weather forecast looked favorable for sailing again.

On Tuesday morning, Buddy was inspecting the mainsail.

"Something wrong?" I asked.

"One of the lazy jacks broke on the mainsail. Probably due to the wind and choppy seas yesterday."

"What is a lazy jack?" Tyler queried.

Buddy replied, "Lazy jacks are lines on the mainsail that are about halfway up the mast. They help keep the mainsail in the right position when raised and lowered from the boom."

"Will that be a problem?" I asked.

Buddy said, "I will need to repair them when we get to Green Turtle Cove. We'll run under power today."

After we stowed everything, we set out to our next destination. Buddy was what he called "putting along" and didn't really need our assistance. "Your jobs today are to sit up on the bow and enjoy the ride."

Tyler and I readily complied. I brought along my reference book about the islands of the Bahamas. Green Turtle Cay is the first island when coming from the Gulf Stream that has a settlement. It is a small island but packed with history. New Plymouth is a small town with restaurants, a post office, a grocery store, a bank, a hardware store and churches - to name a few. There are several marinas, resorts and, of course, beaches. The island is only three miles long. Green Turtle Cay is a place where boaters can stay, waiting for a good weather window to enter Whale Passage into the Atlantic Ocean.

The Sea of Abaco is very shallow between the northern and southern Abaco Islands. For that reason, boaters must go a few miles in the Atlantic Ocean to reach the southern islands. The Whale Pass is known for what is called "the rage" which causes large swells in the waves, and the pass is rocky on both sides. Many people have lost boats to the rage conditions and even loss of life. This is the reason travelers wait for calm seas to cross over.

I turned to Tyler who was soaking up the sun. "Green Turtle Cay sounds like an interesting place to visit. It was settled by English loyalists escaping the Revolutionary War. Some of the architecture has an English flair."

Tyler sat up and replied, "I hope we have time to explore the island."

While we were enjoying the sea breeze and sun, we saw a huge rock to the port side of the boat a good distance way. Buddy was just above us at the helm on the flybridge. "Hey Buddy," I yelled and pointed to the left side of the boat. "What is that huge rock over there?"

Buddy replied, "That is called the 'The Center of the World Rock.' From what I have heard, if one flies over it, the rock has a hole in the center - like a doughnut."

"It's just one of God's wonderful creations," I added.

CHAPTER 18

Green Turtle Cay

The rest of the trip to Green Turtle Cay was uneventful. Because of the size of our boat, Buddy chose a spot at the anchorage at New Plymouth to set the anchor and stow the gear. The boat was equipped with a system that would alarm if the position moved while at anchor. If the boat's anchor became unsecured and started dragging, the boat would shift its position. It was a safety precaution to prevent the boat from drifting and hitting other anchored boats.

Buddy said, "This is a good time for me to repair the lazy jack."

"How do you get up there?" I asked. "It looks like a long climb up the mast."

Buddy laughed, "I don't have to climb up the mast. I have a boson's chair."

"It must be pretty tall," Tyler quipped.

"Here, I'll show you," said Buddy.

We followed him to one of the cockpit compartments, where he produced a harness like one I had seen for rock climbing.

"I slip into this harness, attach it to a line and secure it to a winch," Buddy continued. "I'll grab my tools; and when I'm ready, Tyler, can you assist me by hoisting me up the mast?"

"Certainly," Tyler replied. "Just tell me what to do and when to do it."

When Buddy was ready, I followed them to the mainsail. Buddy secured the halyard to the winch. His tools were in a pouch that was part of the boson's chair. He also had an extra line in case he needed an extra tool.

Once Buddy was prepared for the repair, he instructed Tyler to raise him up a few feet to make sure the boson's seat and straps were secure. Once he felt comfortable, Tyler pulled him slowly to the area of the mainsail so that Buddy could begin the repairs. The operation went smoothly. As Buddy had instructed, Tyler lowered him very slowly back to the deck.

Green Turtle Cay, Abaco

"I'm glad that's over with," Buddy said. "Tyler, you did a great job."

"My pleasure, Buddy," Tyler replied. "I'm glad I was the one on deck!"

Buddy added, "Let me get cleaned up, and we can all go to town. We can take the dinghy into the government docks," pointing to them. "It's a short walk into town."

After securing the dinghy at the dock, Tyler noticed a cannon - just off the rampway. "I wonder how old is that cannon. Hard to tell with all the corrosion."

Buddy answered, "It was salvaged from a sunken ship from the mid-1800s."

We continued our walk down the main street of New Plymouth - lined with brightly colored homes. We passed by the old "gaol" house and several other places of interest. I stopped by the local bakery and purchased a loaf of baked bread. Buddy stopped by the hardware store to pick up some supplies for the boat. Tyler and I bought a couple of T-shirts and a colorful beach towel.

As we were walking back to the dinghy dock, Buddy said, "There is a good restaurant not far from our dinghy. Let's stop for some local cuisine." The local cuisine turned out to be anything made from conch – conch fritters, conch salad, conch stew, to name a few. We met some other cruisers who also were anchored nearby.

It was dusk by the time we boarded the dinghy. We enjoyed the amazing sunset on the way back to the Hodos.

Manjack Cay

It was apparent when we awoke on Thursday morning that we would remain at Green Turtle for another day. Buddy was waiting for a calm day to travel through the Whale Pass into the Atlantic Ocean.

Buddy suggested we visit an uninhabited island nearby, Manjack Cay. Even though the island was a short distance from our anchorage, Buddy decided to pull up the anchor and power to the island. It was shallow near the only wooden dock on the island, so we anchored out in deeper water and took the dinghy ashore.

The Hodos was an impressive boat against the backdrop of the crystal blue water. The wooden dock that extended to the adjoining beach was idyllic - like a scene from a postcard.

"This beach is absolutely beautiful!" I exclaimed. "Look at all the shells! Buddy, is it okay to pick up some shells?"

"Sure, it is. Shelling is a popular pastime on the islands."

I found an empty plastic bag in my backpack and filled it up with an array of shells. We walked the beach for a while enjoying the scenery.

Buddy said, "Over there is a path that will take us to the Atlantic Ocean side of the island. It's a short walk."

The sandy path quickly turned into a dirt path with occasional rocks and sticks. As the path meandered through the thick underbrush, we saw various birds. The path widened and a beautiful white sand beach appeared. The Atlantic Ocean was rough that day, and waves crashed upon the shoreline. As we walked along the beach, there was a gazebo-like structure full of interesting items not far from the beach. "Buddy, what is that?" I asked.

"I don't know how long that has been there, but cruisers clean up the debris washed ashore and place them in there."

Tyler found a Styrofoam ball floating in the water. "I found something to add to the display!"

We walked to the gazebo. Tyler found a loose piece of string and placed the ball on a nail along with an old life jacket.

"Look," I said. "Some of these have writing on them." Further investigation revealed the names of boaters, the names of their vessels and the dates they visited the island.

We found another trail at the base of some palm trees that Buddy said would take us back to the dinghy dock. Along the way, we passed by a couple of houses that were under construction but seemingly abandoned. We assumed the owners had run out of money or were waiting for more building supplies.

We made it back to the boat, powered back to Green Turtle and moored again. The local weather channel on our short band radio said the seas were too rough to cross today. Tyler and I took the dinghy for a ride around the area and stopped at another sailboat moored nearby.

The couple was in the cockpit and waved to us. "May we pull alongside?" Tyler asked.

"Certainly," the man replied. "Throw me a line, and I'll secure it for you."

They were Canadian - Bill and Carla. They had tried to go out into the ocean this morning but decided to return to the harbor - as it was too rough. "We are moving to White Sound for the evening. It will shelter us from the south wind that is coming in tonight," said Bill. We chatted for a while and returned to the Hodos.

Once aboard, Buddy said, "I bought an Abaco Island Wi-Fi subscription. It will give us internet throughout these islands."

"How wonderful!" I exclaimed. "I'll be able to keep up with my family via email!"

"Yes, and it also gives us more extensive weather updates and sea

Dinghy Dock at Manjack Cay, Abaco

conditions," added Buddy.

Tyler told Buddy about the couple we met and their story.

Buddy remarked, "Yes, I have planned to move to the Green Turtle Marina this afternoon. It's in White Sound. In exchange for the dockage, we can have meals at their restaurant, and it will cancel our dock fee!"

Maneuvering through White Sound was a little tricky, with the Hodos being so wide. Fortunately, we waited for high tide and had no real problems getting to the dock. Among the advantages of staying at a marina are that it allows us to refuel, use their facilities for hot showers and meet fellow boaters. During dinner, we met a couple from Maine who stored their boat in dry storage during the fall and winter, moved it to the dock in the summer and traveled around the Abaco Islands in the spring and summer months. What a life! We also met a couple who came to Green Turtle Cove for bone fishing.

Afterward, all of us rented golf carts from the marina and drove to Sundowner's Grill. It would have been faster taking the dinghy, but the golf carts were much more fun!

CHAPTER 20

Great Guana Cay

Since we were ahead of our schedule, Buddy said we could take our time sailing through the Abaco Islands. From what I had read, there were many unique islands to visit along the way.

It seemed like a long time, but we had left St. Marys less than two weeks ago. During breakfast Friday at the marina restaurant, we talked about our upcoming itinerary. Buddy explained, "There are several islands that are worth visiting."

I replied, "I've been looking at the chart book, and it looks like it only takes about two to three hours to island hop."

Tyler added, "I read that there is a ferry that goes to each island in this chain daily. Are we going to take the ferry or sail to each destination?"

Buddy replied, "I thought we could spend a day or two at several islands. That way we would not be limited to the ferry's schedule. Today is a good weather window to cross the Atlantic through Whale Pass. Great Guana Cay is the first island we come to when we re-enter the Sea of Abaco. We will leave this morning, so we'll have more time to explore the island," Buddy explained.

We sailed through the short distance into and out of the Atlantic Ocean with no problem. The Sea of Abaco was calm as well. Buddy decided to pay the dock fee at the government dock in Guana Harbor. Water and power hook-ups were included. It was within walking distance to most of the town.

We considered our options of what to do first. Buddy said, "Pack your swimsuits and a change of clothes. They have a pool, and it's a short walk to the beach."

Shortly thereafter, we walked down the dock and turned left onto Front Street, the only road along Guana Harbor. We strolled past a gift shop, an outdoor restaurant, a bakery, a small grocery store and a church. It was a small, wooden structure - like those I had seen in the country while visiting Virginia. Interestingly, the first settlers here were loyalists from the American Revolution from Virginia and the Carolinas.

Atlantic Ocean side of Great Guana Cay, Abaco

Coming to the end of the storefronts, we turned around and started back down the street. As we walked by the restaurant, I noticed a well-trodden path to one side of the structure. Buddy said, "This is the walkway to Peppers."

It was a wide, sandy path. On either side were bushes and shrubs. The end of the path opened to a parking lot of sorts for bicycles, golf carts and a few vehicles. Peppers had building railings that were painted different bright colors. It had an upper and a lower deck, a bar and two pools. They also had a restaurant and a gift shop. It was built on the edge of a cliff that overlooked the Atlantic Ocean. There was a steep set of wooden stairs that descended to the beach.

"I'm starved," I said. "Buddy, is the food good here?"

"Everything I have tried is delicious."

We entered the restaurant and found a table that overlooked the ocean. The menus were on the table, offering a variety of conch dishes and the usual sandwich, chicken and hamburger plates. When the server came to take our orders, she said the special of the day was fresh-caught tuna - prepared as a sandwich or salad.

I had never had fresh tuna before, so I ordered a tuna sandwich plate that came with French fries and slaw. Tyler and Buddy made their selections - hamburger plates.

"We can get that in the States. Didn't you want to try something new?" I asked.

Tyler said, "I'm not a fan of conch or fish. Hamburger is a sound choice for me."

Buddy said, "I've had so much conch and fish in my sea travels. I'm ready for a good ole' hamburger!"

After lunch, we went down to the Atlantic Ocean and walked on the beach. Again, there was a plethora of shells; and coral washed up on the shore. Shelling was quickly becoming my new hobby. The ocean was a little rough, and I didn't see anyone braving a swim; so we climbed the stairs back to the deck.

"I'd like to go to the pool," I said, "It looks a lot calmer than the ocean."

"I'll join you," said Tyler.

We both had our suits on under our clothes. Since it was Friday afternoon, the two pools were crowded. We chose a pair of beach chairs, laid our belongings down and jumped into the less crowded pool. Buddy remained on the deck, talking to some old friends.

The establishment had live music that night, so we stayed for a while and enjoyed meeting some fellow boaters. We left early because we did not want to walk back to the boat in the dark.

CHAPTER 21

Paradise Bay

On Saturday morning, after breakfast, I said, "I think I'll sit out on the forward deck and relax." Tyler tagged along.

While soaking up the sun, I was browsing my travel book about the Abaco Islands. "Tyler, did you know there was an exclusive resort on the far side of the island?"

"No, I didn't know that. What does it say about it?"

I continued, "It's called Paradise Bay. It has only been open a year. It's a planned community for the super-rich and famous people."

Tyler asked, "Like movie stars and sports figures?"

"Yes," I replied. "And anyone who can afford multimillion dollar lots, not counting the cost of construction of a home."

"Let's rent a golf cart in town, and look around the island," Tyler offered.

After telling Buddy our plans, we walked to the facility that rented golf carts. The island is only about nine miles long. The only main road was paved to the other end of the island. Vacation houses were dotted among the Bahamian Coppice shrubs. We reached the entrance to Baker's Bay. There was a guard at the gate to the entrance. "Do you have business here?" he asked.

Tyler said, in his distinct English accent, "We are interested in looking at your lots for sale."

"Do you have an appointment?" the guard queried.

"No, we are visiting the island; and we thought we could get a tour of the community."

The guard said, "One moment please." He entered the gate house and made a phone call. Shortly, he returned and said, "Follow me, and I will take you to the sales office."

"Thank you," Tyler said.

The guard walked to his security golf cart with the "Paradise Bay" logo. We followed through the development. We passed several massive homes and some that were under construction around the golf course. The guard parked his cart and pointed to a space for us to park as well. He said, "Here is the real estate office. Mr. Michaels will be waiting for you."

When the guard drove away, I asked Tyler, "What are we going to say when we meet the salesman?"

"Let me do the talking, and you just go along with me," Tyler said.

Mr. Michaels met us at the door, and Tyler introduced ourselves. Mr. Michaels wore an expensive-looking, tailored suit. He motioned us to a room with a large map of the community on the wall. He said, "We opened last year; and as you probably saw, several homes are completed." The map was comprised of several subdivisions, including estate lots, beach cottages and flats. Some were along the coastline - inland facing the golf course.

"What are the costs of these lots?" Tyler asked.

Mr. Michaels replied, "The lots vary in price, according to their location. What are you interested in?"

Tyler and I looked at the options; and Tyler stated, "We are looking for a smaller lot - a place we could come for holiday."

Mr. Michaels circled a few of the available lots and said, "These beach cottage lots are the smallest. They range from $100,000 to $800,000." He provided a brochure which included a map of the island and the lots available. "Here is my business card. Let me know when you make a decision."

Tyler thanked him, and they shook hands. We left the building, got into the golf cart and rode back to the entrance. We thanked the guard for helping us. After we left the property, I said to Tyler, "How did you come up with that plan?"

Tyler answered, "I knew the only way we could look around Paradise Bay would be to say we were interested in buying a lot."

"But wasn't that deceptive?"

"Not really," Tyler replied. "I was interested in the price of a lot; and if I had the money, I'd buy a lot. Just think, they have been open only a year; and there are plenty of lots available. If one were to buy a lot, who knows what it would sell for in 10 years? It could prove to be quite an investment."

We drove back to town, turned in our golf cart and walked back to the boat. For once, Buddy was resting on the trampoline at the bow of the boat. We told him about our adventure to Paradise Bay.

"I've never been over there," Buddy said. "It's too fancy for my taste, but I'm glad you had a good time."

Yawning, I said, "It has been a big day. I think I'll just have a salad for supper and turn in early." Tyler and Buddy ate supper with me and then selected a movie.

After showering, I laid down on my bed, realizing I had not been faithful in my daily devotions. I caught up with the past few days of reading until I fell asleep.

CHAPTER 22

Relaxation and Revelation

The next morning, Tyler and I decided to walk to the little church that we had seen yesterday on Front Street. We asked Buddy if he wanted to go; and surprisingly, he agreed. The Guana Cay Community Church was a small wooden structure. The church was part of the Abaco missionary churches. Pastors from multiple denominations from the States would travel the Abaco Islands and from one island to the other to preach on a rotation basis.

The congregation consisted of some residents as well as transient boaters. Buddy said that he enjoyed visiting the island churches because there was a more relaxed atmosphere than churches he had visited back home.

After the service was over, we strolled back to the boat. Buddy said, "Let's have lunch on the boat today. I thought I would grill some chicken breasts. Aspen, could you prepare a salad?"

"Certainly," I replied. I had stocked up on some fresh vegetables and a fresh loaf of baked bread from the local grocery. "I'll make some garlic bread as well."

While Buddy was still on the bow grilling the chicken, I said to Tyler, "Since Buddy went to church with us, let's try to talk to him over lunch."

Tyler replied, "I'll try to start a conversation."

As I finished setting the table in the cockpit, Buddy returned from the bow with the grilled chicken. We sat down and Tyler said a prayer, giving thanks to God for the food and blessing us so far in our journey. Then he said, "I am so happy that I decided to return to church."

"How so?" asked Buddy.

Tyler continued, "As I was talking to Aspen after we attended church in St. Marys, I grew up in a Christian family. I received Jesus as my Savior at a young age and was baptized. My parents died in an automobile accident when I was in high school. I went to live with my Uncle Allen who had a gambling addiction. After his work, I was left home alone while he caroused in a local pub. He was not a good influence on me. I quit going to church because Uncle Allen would make fun of me and say I was weak. He was a selfish man, wanting me to depend on him. In secret, I did continue to read my Bible and pray at bedtime. When I graduated from high school, l left home to University. My friends invited me to go to campus church. I rededicated my life to Christ and became involved in church activities."

Buddy said, "Thanks for sharing. I guess I can tell my situation. My family lived in Atlanta. My parents were believers, and we attended Presbyterian church. I considered myself a Christian because I was christened when I was a baby. To join the church, when children turned 13, a class was held on the book of Catechism. I had to memorize the questions and answers in that book about the fundamental beliefs of a Christian. Upon completion of the class, one Sunday, the graduates of the class were called to the front of the church, and we professed our belief in Jesus."

Buddy continued, "After graduating from college, I worked as a computer programmer. I met Harvey at a convention, and we became friends. One day he invited me to his Baptist church. I knew there was a man who attended there, who had been a teacher in my high school. That former teacher was accused of dishonorable conduct and was fired. I thanked Harvey for inviting me and told him I could not attend a church that had hypocrites. Harvey said that the man had confessed his sin before the church and asked for forgiveness. I said I didn't care, I wasn't going to his church, and I asked Harvey not to take offense. I wanted to remain friends with him."

"Is that the reason you didn't want to go to the Baptist church in St. Marys?" I asked.

"Unfortunately, yes," he replied. "Since then, I have been researching Scriptures online. I found out something that made a difference for me. In 2 Corinthians, Paul says in chapter 5, verses 16 and 17, 'So we have stopped evaluating others from a human point of view. At one time we thought of Christ merely from a human point of view. How differently we know him now! This means that anyone who belongs to Christ has become a new person. The old life is gone; a new life has begun!' I see your faith; and I feel that way, too."

"That is wonderful, Buddy!" I exclaimed. "Praise the Lord!"

"I realize that I had head knowledge of Christ; but now I admit that I am a sinner, that Christ died for my sins, that I am forgiven and that Christ is in my heart." Buddy added, "When I get back to Atlanta, I am going to apologize to Harvey and see if I can be baptized in his church."

Tyler said, "I am so proud of you. Welcome to the family of believers!"

After cleaning up, we decided to go back to Peppers, enjoy another day at the pool and another walk along the beach and look for more seashells. We walked back through the town. The ferry boat had just docked. We sat on a park bench and watched people disembark - mostly locals probably returning home from employment at other local islands. Obviously, it was the last shuttle of the day because the boat left with no passengers. Then we returned to the boat. Buddy had been relaxing on the trampoline on the bow of the boat. He greeted us, looked at his watch and said, "Let's walk over to Grabber's Grill. Maybe we can catch an early dinner before it gets crowded."

"Do we have time to shower and change clothes?" I asked.

Buddy replied, "Sure"; and he pointed, "It is just over there - hardly a stone's throw from the entrance to the dock."

Grabbers had a pool and an outdoor area for dining. There were several rental cabins on the property. We placed our order and found an open picnic table, facing the waterfront.

View of Elbow Reef Lighthouse from the Hodos, Elbow Cay, Abaco

There were some people playing an unfamiliar game in a sandy court with what looked like croquet balls. I asked Buddy, "Do you know what game they are playing over there?"

"It's an Italian game called bocce ball."

"Looks like fun," Tyler said.

Buddy replied, "We can walk over there after dinner and see if we can join in."

I asked Buddy, "Can you explain the game to us?"

"Simply put, the game is usually played by two opposing teams. Each player has two throwing balls of the same color. The team takes turns throwing the small, white ball - called a pallina - across a midcourt line. The players take turns throwing the larger balls to see who comes closest to the smaller ball. The object of the game is to get your thrown ball closer to the pallina than the opposing team."

After paying for our meals, we ambled over to the bocce ball court and watched the current game. At the end of the game, the winners asked if there were any challengers. Tyler and I stepped forward. One of the winners wanted to take a break and asked Buddy to fill in for him. It was obvious that Buddy had played before. They beat us fair and square. We did have a good time though.

We hung around to watch the fabulous sunset. I wondered why the owners named this place Grabbers because Sunset Grill seemed more appropriate. We strolled back to the boat - clearly spent from a long, interesting day.

CHAPTER 23

Marsh Harbor

On Monday morning, over breakfast, Buddy said, "It's been fun, but it's time to island hop to Marsh Harbor."

Tyler asked, "How long will it take for us to get there?"

"At seven knots per hour, it will take about an hour."

"These islands of Abaco are pretty close together," I said.

Buddy added, "It is nice not to have to get up every morning at the break of dawn to travel from one island to another."

We took our time getting ready to sail and left Guana Harbor shortly after lunch.

The weather and seas were perfect to cross over to Marsh Harbor. The weather was warm but windy. There were quite a few boats in the anchorage. Buddy said, "This is an excellent anchorage. The harbor is sheltered from three sides."

After we anchored, Tyler and Buddy lowered the dinghy and went to the government docks. Buddy had to buy a couple of new batteries and told us we could look around town. Tyler went with him.

I crossed the street and entered a local boutique. While browsing, I found some local, handmade pocketbooks made from weaved palm fronds. I made my selection and went to the register to pay. There was another woman at the register, paying for her purchase. I overheard the lady behind the desk ask her where she was from. "North Carolina," she said.

I chimed in, "I'm from Georgia. My name is Aspen."

"I'm Val," she responded. "It's a small world, isn't it?"

"Are you moored in the anchorage?" I asked.

"No, we are docked at the marina," Val replied.

We chatted a few minutes upon leaving the shop. She and her husband sailed around the Abaco Islands every year. "We are having dinner at the marina restaurant tonight. Won't you join us?"

"Well, there are three of us onboard our sailboat."

Val replied, "We will be there around 7 p.m. Come if you can."

We went our separate ways, and I returned to the dinghy.

We made it to the restaurant on time. I saw Val and waved to her. She and her husband Will were seated at a larger table. I introduced her to Tyler and Buddy as we sat down.

Val said, "We met a couple of sailors at our dock and invited them to join us as well."

A few minutes later, two young men arrived. I figured they were in their 20s. One had shaggy blonde hair, and the other one had nicely trimmed black hair. The shaggy haired guy spoke, "Sorry we are late. We caught some mackerel this afternoon, and the chef is preparing it for our table."

"How thoughtful of you, Judson," Val said. "I'd like you to meet Aspen, Tyler and Buddy. They are on a catamaran in the harbor."

"Hi, I'm Judson; and this is my friend Zach," replied the guy with the shaggy hair.

We exchanged pleasantries and how each of our itineraries brought us together. Judson had just graduated from MIT. He owned an internet company and recently sold it to take a year off and sail around the Caribbean. Zach was his childhood friend. They were both from Florida.

The blackened mackerel was delicious. It was too spicy for me, and I paid for it the rest of the night. Good thing I brought along antacid pills.

The next morning, over breakfast, Buddy said, "I need to repair a frayed reef line. I hope to find some sewing needles in town. There are a couple of portable bicycles on the boat. Will told me at dinner last night that they also had a couple of bikes. Would ya'll like to ride into town with me?"

"Sure, we would," Tyler replied.

"How are we going to get the bikes to shore?" I asked.

Buddy said, "We'll load them up in the dinghy and power to dock.

"How are we going to get a bicycle from Will?" Tyler queried.

"I texted Will, and he will meet us at the dinghy dock with a bike."

Marsh Harbor is part of the Great Abaco Island and large enough to have its own airport. There are paved roads through the town. As we rode down Bay Street, we passed a bank and a pharmacy before we turned away from the harbor onto Don Mackey Boulevard. Buddy first stopped at a marine store and then a hardware store for some provisions. I almost felt like I was at home during our shopping excursion.

On the way to the grocery store, I spotted a post office. I had a couple of cards that I had been waiting to mail somewhere. Next door was an ice cream shop. As Buddy and Tyler parked their bikes, Tyler said, "What flavor of ice cream do you want?"

"Chocolate," I replied. I bought the local stamps and mailed the cards. Upon returning to the ice cream shop, I found Tyler and Buddy at a table enjoying their frozen treats. After a break in the air conditioning, we continued to the grocery store.

As we got to the parking lot, it was packed with cars. "I wonder why there is such a crowd at the market on a Tuesday?" I asked.

Once inside, we found out this was the grand opening of this store, featuring a great deal of items on sale. We took advantage of the sales and stocked up on some canned goods and fresh baked bread. Fortunately, our bikes had ample baskets for the groceries.

Riding a bike was a little scary for me, having to use the British side of riding on the left along narrow roads and not many sidewalks. A couple of times, we had to stop and wait for oncoming traffic to clear.

We made it safely back to the dinghy dock. Will and Val met us there to retrieve their bicycle. We chatted a few minutes and returned to the Hodos.

As Buddy repaired the frayed reef line, Tyler and I put up the groceries. After lunch, we boarded the dinghy again and drove across the harbor to a sandwich shop. After lunch, we walked a couple of blocks to Mermaid Beach and walked along the rock shoreline. After picking up a few shells, we returned to the dinghy and rode around the harbor, looking at all the different boats that were moored.

There was one trawler that had an aft mast. At night, it lit up with a string of blue lights. I remember seeing those lights from our boat at night. It started sprinkling just as Buddy and Tyler secured the dinghy.

After dinner, Buddy listened to the local weather station. He said, "I wanted to cross over to the Eleuthera Islands tomorrow, but there's a storm with high winds brewing that way. So I've made a change of plans. We'll stay in the Abaco Islands and wait for a suitable weather window. I think we'll go to Hopetown tomorrow."

"How far is Hopetown from Marsh Harbor?" I asked.

"It's another short jump. We can leave after breakfast and get there in a couple of hours."

I was exhausted from the activities of the day. I turned in early and caught up on reading my Bible before falling asleep.

Man removing conch shell, Marsh Harbor, Abaco

CHAPTER 24

Elbow Cay

The next morning, after breakfast, we set sail to Elbow Cay, Hope-town, to be exact. The main part of this town surrounds a pro-tected harbor. As we approached the narrow inlet, we couldn't help but see the candy cane-striped lighthouse overlooking the harbor. Buddy and Tyler had no trouble mooring our vessel. Tyler asked, "Bud-dy, do you want me to set the positional alarm?"

"No, when we have a line attached to a mooring buoy, it is not nec-essary. The ground tackle is heavy enough not to drift."

The day was young. I asked, "Can we go up in that lighthouse?"

"Sure can," replied Buddy. "Let's lower the dinghy, and go over to see it."

We tied up at the dinghy dock and walked a short distance to the Elbow Reef Lighthouse. It was 89 feet tall. Once inside, there was a spi-ral staircase. We made it up the 101 steps. The last few steps were quite steep. At the top of the lighthouse was the room with the Fresnel lenses. We walked out onto the viewing area. The view was spectacular. The strip of houses on the peninsula and boats in the harbor made it look like a toy city. The view extended out to the ocean. Upon leaving the lighthouse, I picked up a pamphlet from the gift shop. Built around 1883, it is the only hand-wound, nonelectric, kerosene-burning lighthouse left today in the world. Due to the location of the lighthouse, its light can be seen from 23 nautical miles from the Sea of Abaco and the Atlantic Ocean.

While walking back to the dinghy, Buddy said, "I'm hungry! I know a place in the main village where we can grab some lunch." Tyler and I agreed. On the other side of the harbor was a colorful building with a place to tie up the dinghy.

Captain Jack's Restaurant was a white building with pink trim. We selected a table on the deck. Buddy ordered conch fritters as an appetizer. I selected a Caesar salad with chicken. Tyler decided to try the Anthea Burger (made by the owner's mother), and Buddy chose the chicken burger.

"Let's take a walk," I offered.

Buddy added, "There are a lot of interesting places on the island."

The houses had a variety of colorful paint. We walked past a two-story, light-green house with white trim and pink shutters The next house was also two-story - white with green trim. In the front yard, there was a small replica of the house next to a pond. "Look at that cute, little house," I said.

Buddy answered, "That is a lizard house. There are lots of lizards on the island."

Tyler pointed, "I see one! Look at the curly tail!"

The next point of interest on the main street was a Methodist Church. It was white with bright, yellow shutters on the windows. The rear of the church faced the Atlantic Ocean. Past the church was a walkway to the ocean. At the entrance stood a little pavilion with beach wash finds - mostly a various assortment of buoys.

At this point, we crossed over to the other side of the street, where there was an ice cream shop. Again, it was a two-story building that was painted dark pink with blue trim. "I'm ready for a cone of ice cream," I said. The guys agreed. We ordered our cones and went upstairs to a lovely deck with tables and colorful umbrellas.

As we were leaving, Buddy said, "Let's rent a golf cart, and take a ride to the other side of the island." The golf cart had two seats facing forward and two seats facing backward. I sat next to Buddy, and Tyler took the back seat.

We drove through a more commercial side of town. "Can we stop at the art gallery?" I asked.

Lizard house, Hopetown, Abaco

Buddy pulled into a parking spot and said, "I'll wait on you while you check it out."

"Tyler, do you want to come with me?"

"No, I'll wait with Buddy."

I grabbed my wallet and walked up to the brightly colored building. The gallery had a section of local artists. My eye caught a small lithograph of the Elbow Reef Lighthouse. On the reverse side of the canvas was a photograph of the artist and a paragraph about her. This was a perfect souvenir of our visit to Elbow Cay. I made my purchase and trotted back to the golf cart.

Tyler asked, "Did you find anything?"

"Yes," I answered and showed him the picture.

"That is really nice," he said.

Buddy agreed, started the golf cart and backed out of the parking spot. We drove through the lower part of the island on a well-paved road, paralleling the ocean.

"Are we going anywhere in particular?" I asked.

Buddy replied, "Tahiti Beach."

"Sounds exotic," I said.

It didn't take long to get to the south side of the island. There was a marina near the beach, and we were able to park there. When we reached the beach, it was low tide. There was a beautiful white sandbar with the Caribbean crystal-clear blue water on each side. The beach side was lined with palm trees.

Tyler and I removed our sandals and waded through the shallow water to the sandbar. There were a few people there. To our left, a couple of children were flying kites. Another family had anchored their dinghy and were frolicking in the water. We turned to look at the shore; and to our surprise, Buddy had brought some beach towels and was motioning for us to meet him.

Tyler and I splashed through the water along the beach.

"I brought some drinks and snacks," Buddy said.

As we sat down on the beach towels, I said, "How thoughtful! Thank you!"

We relaxed on the beach and enjoyed the warm sun and mild breeze until the tide began to roll in. Tyler and I helped Buddy pack up, and we walked back to the golf cart.

After reaching the north side of the island, we returned the cart, walked back to the courtesy dock and took the dinghy back to the boat.

The afternoon turned into twilight; and after dinner, we sat out on the bow of the sailboat, enjoying the sunset. A gentleman putted by in his dinghy on his way to his sailboat and stopped to say hello. We introduced ourselves and began chatting with John. We were talking about how we loved seeing the dolphins swim with us as we were under sail. John was sailing solo on his way back to the States.

He told us the most unusual story. He said, "I was anchored out one night offshore. Just before sunrise, I heard a banging noise at the bow of the boat. I ventured out on the deck to investigate. There was a dolphin struggling to get free from a fishing net. I changed into swimming trunks and gathered my life vest, mask, snorkel and flippers. I grabbed my knife and slipped into the water from the swim ladder. I slowly swam to the bow. The animal appeared fatigued; and I was afraid that if I didn't free the dolphin, he would die.

"Moving closer, I gently stroked his side. The dolphin did not resist. Then I began carefully cutting the net around him. I freed one fin and then another. While I was working, two curious dolphins swam up to the boat and circled the trapped dolphin. I continued freeing the net until the dolphin was liberated. The dolphin nuzzled me in the side before swimming off with his buddies."

"That's a fascinating story!" I exclaimed.

Buddy added, "Dolphins are very intelligent."

"Yes," John said. "I will never forget the experience."

Tyler stated, "Thank you for sharing your story."

"I enjoyed our time together, but I need to get back to the boat before dark," John said.

Buddy said the weather and sea conditions were going to be favorable for the next couple of days. He said, "Tomorrow we'll sail to Little Harbor Cay. We will stay there tomorrow night and leave early the next morning for our jump to Eleuthera."

I looked at the chart of the area. "Looks like it will take us only a couple of hours to get there."

"Yes," Buddy replied. "We'll leave after breakfast and spend the day there."

Tyler, who liked to read the travel books, said, "It says here there is an art gallery there."

"That is true. I hope it's open on Thursdays," Buddy remarked.

It had been an exciting day exploring Hopetown and the island. I was exhausted and turned in early. Before going to sleep, I prayed and thanked God for the beauty of Elbow Cay and for safe travels to Eleuthera.

CHAPTER 25

Little Harbor

We left early the next morning because Buddy said there was limited space in the sheltered anchorage at Little Harbor. We sailed without any problems. Tyler and I lowered the sails as we approached the entrance to the harbor. Buddy idled the engines and said, "This channel has depth of about three feet at high tide. Go to the bow and watch the depth for me."

Buddy slowly maneuvered the boat between the channel markers. "Looks like there is plenty of room to anchor," Tyler said.

"It's a good thing we left early. This harbor fills up fast," Buddy responded. Buddy found a spot to moor. The anchor set well in the grassy bottom. After things were squared away, Buddy lowered the dinghy, and we powered over to the courtesy dock. We strolled along the beach. Close to the shoreline were curious rock formations. Between the cracks and crevices were clusters of small seashells. I picked an unusual rock and said to Tyler, "Look at this flat rock. It's shaped like half of a sandwich."

Tyler had gathered a couple of shells as well. I found some broken conch shells. "The insides are twisted in a spiral shape."

I always wore a small backpack when we walked along the beach. We combined our finds and placed them in a zippered compartment.

Buddy walked with us and pointed to a boardwalk that connected to a deck and that led to a unique, open-air restaurant. It was constructed from an old boat. The rafters were covered with T-shirts donated by boaters over the years. There were brightly colored picnic tables for dining. We placed our orders. To pass the time, I pulled out the assortment. When the server brought our food, she asked about the flat rock. "That looks like a sandwich! We have an assortment of oddities at our bar. Would you like to donate your rock?"

"Certainly," I replied.

"Thank you."

When we went to the bar to check out, there was the rock. The waitress had painted it with colored markers, and now it really did resemble a sandwich!

Buddy said, "Let's walk over to the Atlantic Ocean side of the island."

There was another boardwalk leading to the beach. The sandy terrain had a scattering of underbrush, small shrubs and trees. From the branches of one tree hung various flip-flops and sandals. It turned out this was called the shoe tree. The shoes that had washed ashore hung there.

Next we stopped by the art gallery. The founding settlers of the island created a bronze foundry. They make unique statues and sculptures. Family members have continued to live on the island, and they maintain the art gallery and restaurant. They have unique items such as fish and birds, but the prices were way out of my price range!

It had been another wonderful day. I thought about the beauty of the Abaco Islands as we ferried the dinghy back to our home at sea. Once settled on board, Buddy called us into the salon. "Starting early tomorrow morning, we'll make our jump across the Atlantic Ocean. Our next destination is Royal Island. It's at the northern tip of the Eleuthera Island chain."

"How long will it take us to get there?" I asked.

Tyler plotted the course on the chart. "My estimation is about 10 hours. The sea conditions are favorable."

Buddy added, "Royal Island is privately owned. That means that we'll be unable to go ashore."

Flip Flop tree, Little Harbor, Abaco

CHAPTER 26

Eleuthera

Just before sunrise, we pulled up the anchor and idled through the channel toward the Atlantic Ocean. It was a beautiful day, with calm seas and a light wind that was just right for sailing. Because it was an all-day trip, Buddy let Tyler and me take turns sailing the Hodos. We were able to use the autopilot a good deal of the time.

The anchorage on Royal Island was an excellent spot to anchor because it was sheltered from the wind from almost all sides. There were a few sailboats already there when we arrived about 6:30 p.m.

I noticed a trawler with a blue string of lights on its aft mast.

"We saw that boat at Marsh Harbor," I said. "I remember the blue lights."

Tyler said, "I remember its name was Eternity."

"Do we have time to take the dinghy over and meet them?" I queried.

"Sure," Buddy replied. "Tyler, will you help me with the dinghy?"

Tyler nodded. Shortly after that, we rode over to the trawler.

There was an older couple sitting on the foredeck. Buddy came alongside and said, "Hello, we are anchored over there in the catamaran."

The gentleman said, "Hi there. Let me throw you a line, and you can tie up and come aboard."

We secured the line and climbed the ladder to his trawler.

The skipper said, "I'm Hank, and this is my wife Sarah."

"I am Buddy, and Tyler and Aspen are my crew," he spoke.

"I think we saw your trawler at Marsh Harbor a few days ago. I remember the blue string of lights on your aft mass," I explained.

Hank replied, "Yes. I think I remember your catamaran."

"Where are you headed?" Sarah asked.

Buddy answered, "We are delivering the boat to its owner in Georgetown."

Hank said, "That is our destination as well. This is our first trip to the Exumas. Would you mind if we travel with you?"

"No, not at all," Buddy answered. "We are leaving in the morning for the gas docks at Spanish Wells. We'll be back after lunch. We will head out to the Exumas the next morning bright and early. You're welcome to join us if you can wait until Sunday."

"Sarah and I will discuss our plans and let you know tomorrow when you return from Spanish Wells."

Buddy said, "We'll touch base with you tomorrow then."

They helped us with our lines, and we rode back to our boat.

Over dinner, Buddy said, "I think you will like Spanish Wells. It's a unique village."

"I look forward to it," I replied.

We played a game of dominoes before turning in for the night. I enjoyed taking a day off between long crossings between islands.

It took less than one hour to reach Spanish Wells. The Hodos had no trouble entering the long waterway strip. The gas dock was not far from the entrance of the harbor. Buddy said the diesel gas prices were reasonable. Since there were not many boaters gassing up, the owner let us tie up at the lower end of the dock and we walked into town for lunch. The main street was lined with colorful houses - like the ones we saw at Elbow Cay. Most of the families on St. George's Cay are fishermen. The town supplies lobsters for the Red Lobster Restaurant chain.

After lunch, we headed back to Royal Island. Once anchored, Buddy invited Hank and Sarah over for dinner. Hank caught some lobster earlier that day, and Sarah made a wonderful lobster dip and chips. Tyler cooked hamburgers on the grill, and I made a salad.

During our meal, Buddy discussed our next step of our journey. "Not far from Royal Island is Current Cut, which is a short cut to the Exumas. This narrow strip of water is between Royal Island and Current Island."

"Why is it called Current Cut?" Tyler asked.

Buddy replied, "Depending on the tides, the currents can be up to 10 knots. If a captain is not cautious, his vessel will get caught in an eddy."

Hank said, "Sarah and I decided, if it's okay with you, we would like to sail with you to the Exumas. It's best to go with an experienced boater who knows how to travel through the current."

"We'll be glad to have you join us," Buddy continued. "After traversing though the cut, we have to cross the Yellow Bank. It is filled with coral heads - many just below the waterline. One wrong move and the sharp coral head can rip a boat's hull wide open."

"Just tell us what to do, and we'll follow your lead," Hank said.

"After crossing the bank, we"ll moor at Allen's Cay overnight. Again, it's tricky to enter the cove; but if the weather holds, it's a good shelter," Buddy said.

Sarah said, "We are so grateful to travel with you. I have been anxious about our crossing safely to the Exumas."

I asked, "How long will it take us to get to Allen's Cay?"

"If the sea and weather conditions are favorable - about eight hours," Buddy replied.

Hank asked, "What time will we shove off in the morning?"

"Let's leave about 9 a.m. That will allow us time to reach the Yellow Bank about midday, and the sun should be straight over head," Buddy added.

Hank and Sarah left shortly after dinner. Tyler and I cleaned up the galley and salon. Buddy turned in early. Tyler and I watched a movie before retiring to our respective bunks.

CHAPTER 27

Cautious Crossing to the Exumas

On Sunday, we pulled up anchor and idled away from the anchorage about 9:30 a.m. The Eternity followed us out of the inlet. Buddy kept in touch with Hank with the VHF marine radio. "Hank, be sure you are under power while we traverse the cut."

Buddy said, "We are almost to the channel. Tyler, set a waypoint on the chart plotter. Once we enter the channel, set a course of 130 degrees."

"Aye, Captain."

There were two islands on either side of the channel. I could see the change in the current ahead of us.

Buddy said, "Aspen, help me watch our course; and let me know if we veer off the center of the channel."

Deftly steering, Buddy followed the channel eastward and then cut starboard southward.

"I see rocks on either side, Buddy!"

Buddy replied, "We should be fine as long as we stay in the center of the channel. The depth in the middle of the channel is 40 feet."

We exited the channel and waited for Hank and Sarah to catch up. They had followed our course with no problems.

"What a roller coaster ride that was!" I exclaimed.

"That is nothing compared to our next segment through Yellow Bank," Buddy replied.

Hank and Sarah pulled up alongside. Tyler and I secured fenders between the boats. Buddy discussed the plan for crossing the coral heads. "We will remain under power and just at about five knots. Sarah, you will keep watch at the bow of your boat; and Aspen will keep watch on our boat. I will tiptoe around the coral heads, and you follow my course. Even at high tide, some spots over the coral heads are only about three feet."

I prayed silently that God would protect us and allow us safe passage through the Yellow Bank.

We began our trek slowly through the labyrinth of coal heads. Buddy said the coral heads were best seen in broad daylight; they are virtually undetectable if there is cloud cover. It was a blessing that we had a sunny day.

Standing watch at the bow, whenever I saw a blackish/gray shape just beneath the waterline, I shouted out, "There's one" and would point in the appropriate direction. It was a painstaking mine field, taking us four hours to clear the maze of coral heads.

Not long after we left the Yellow Bank, I saw an island in the distance. "I see land!" I exclaimed, pointing starboard.

Tyler added, "We've made it to the Exumas!"

Buddy said, "That is a cluster of three islands called Allen's Cay. If it's not too crowded with boaters, we will anchor there tonight."

On the VHS radio, Buddy hailed the Eternity and conveyed our plans to anchor there tonight. The main entrance to the harbor split between two islands. The longer island to port was lined with anchored vessels. Straight ahead was a smaller island with only a few boats moored. Buddy found a suitable spot and secured the Hodos. Eternity anchored close by.

Clearly, we were all exhausted from our strenuous journey. It was just past 5 p.m. I made sandwiches, and we ate dinner in the cockpit and talked about the adventurous day. Buddy said, "These islands are the only place in the world where these particular species of iguanas inhabit," pointing to the nearest island to our stern.

"I thought iguanas lived in many places around the world," I said.

"Not the Northern Bahamian Rock Iguanas," Buddy replied. "There are subspecies that are found on Andros Island and Exuma Island.

Tyler asked, "Do we have time to go ashore tomorrow?"

"Yes," replied Buddy. "We'll go over to Leaf Island in the morning before the tourists from Nassau come for their shore excursion."

"Tourists in Nassau pay to come here?" I asked.

Tyler quipped, "Too bad they can't crew on a sailboat and visit for free!"

When the wind picked up during the night, the catamaran rocked and rolled. Even though the anchor held, I did not sleep well. By morning, the sea was calm again. After breakfast, we took the dinghy ashore.

The iguanas were already out, warming up from the sun on the beach. Buddy told us not to feed them anything as they can be aggressive between each other over food. We found a path and wandered through the island. An occasional iguana slipped out from the underbrush. We did not bother them, and they did not bother us.

We came to an old concrete wall that was covered in graffiti by tourists and boaters. I asked Buddy if he knew anything about the ruins, but he didn't know its origins. The path ended on the far side of the island, facing the Exuma Sound. The bare beach was pristine against the turquoise water.

When we returned to our dinghy, a large tour excursion powerboat was idling by the shore. There must have been 50 tourists on board. One of the tour guides was passing bags to the people. "What is he doing?" I asked Buddy.

"They are passing out bags of fruit to feed the iguanas."

Iguanas at Allen's Cay, Exuma

We boarded our dinghy and pulled away from shore. About that time, a barrage of tourists hustled to shore, tossing bits of fruit to the iguanas. Several of the large reptiles charged the food. As they fought for a morsel, several of the women screamed and ran back to the beached boat. I was glad we left when we did!

Once back on the catamaran, Buddy hailed Hank on the radio. He explained that we were leaving for Big Major's Spot after lunch and asked if they would travel with us. They were thankful for the invitation and were ready to leave.

CHAPTER 28

Big Major's Spot

Exuma consists of 365 islands. Between Allen's Cay and Big Major's Spot are at least 17 cays. Our schedule did not permit Buddy to stop at every location. Unless we were waiting for a good weather window to continue our journey, we usually sailed a good part of the day to get to the next destination. The sea and wind conditions were favorable today. Under smooth, open sail at seven knots, our trip took about five hours from Allen's Cay to reach Big Major's Spot. Buddy wanted to stop there because of the special attraction there.

The anchorage at Big Major's Spot was sandy. It was about six to nine feet deep, depending on the tide. Buddy said it would protect us from the north, east and southeast winds. Since there were only a few boats moored here, there was plenty of room for the Hodos and the Eternity to anchor.

Buddy said, "Let's take the dinghy to the beach."

About halfway to the beach, I noticed several large pigs - one tan-colored and one that had black-and-white spots - on the shoreline. "Look at those pigs!" About that time, the pigs got into the water and swam to our dinghy. "I didn't know pigs could swim."

Buddy explained, "Another name for this island is Pig Island. About 20 to 30 feral pigs live here."

"How did they get here?" Tyler asked.

"No one knows for sure. Some say there was a shipwreck, and the pigs swam to shore."

"They seem friendly," I added.

"They are hoping we have some food for them."

We beached the dinghy and walked up and down the beach, with the pigs walking with us. I found a few shells. Buddy said, "Take the dinghy and ride around. There are several small islands and rock formations that might be of interest. Just drop me off at the boat."

Pig swimming to the dinghy at Big Major's Spot, Exuma

"Thanks, Buddy. That sounds like fun."

We walked back to the dinghy, took Buddy to the boat and rode up the shoreline. The sandy beach turned into a forest of shrubs and undergrowth. The shoreline was now rocky with limestone formations that were sharp and jaggy and loomed about three feet over the waterline. Traveling a little farther around the island, sand reappeared. There were large boulders dotting the beach. Somehow a determined tree grew from the top of the large rock. As we steered away from the island, around the end were rock islands. There was no beach. However, we did manage to beach the dinghy on a smooth portion of the rock surface. There were a lone tree and underbrush toward the middle of the island. One little area of the rock island had some sand mixed in the small black rock formations. Here was an abundance of small seashells and coral.

The sun was setting over the group of rock islands. "Tyler, look at that spectacular sunset!"

"Where did the time go?" he responded. "I think we better get back to the boat. I don't want Buddy to think we got lost!"

The ride back to the boat was marvelous, watching the beauty of God's handiwork.

Buddy was standing out on the bow when we returned. He traversed over to the cockpit to help us step out of the dinghy. "I was starting to worry. Did you have any trouble with the engine?"

"No. We enjoyed exploring the area, and time slipped away," Tyler explained.

"When we saw the breathtaking sunset, we realized how late it was," I added.

"Well, I'm glad you're back. Hank and Sarah have invited us to dinner. They're having spaghetti, and I prepared a salad." So we all returned to the dinghy and went over to Hank and Sarah's.

During dinner, Buddy said, "The sea conditions on Tuesday are going to be choppy and windy and not a good day to sail. Since our inlet provides a good shelter, we'll remain here another day."

Hank asked, "Would it be possible for us to go by dinghy to Staniel Cay and see the Thunderball Grotto?"

"Let's see what the weather is like here tomorrow."

It was getting late, and again we had a long but good day. I certainly would not mind staying at this lovely island another day.

CHAPTER 29

Thunderball Grotto

When I awoke the next morning, the sun was shining brightly. After breakfast, Tyler and I decided to jump into the water. I took several foam swim noodles and floated in the crystal-clear water. I floated around to the bow of the boat, holding on to the anchor line. Tyler dove into the water, came up next to me and started splashing water. We playfully sprayed each other. Buddy was standing on the bow of the boat and said, "Don't panic, but slowly swim back to the swim ladder."

"Why?" I asked.

"Just swim back, and I'll show you."

Of course, I panicked, trying to swim back to the stern. Tyler grabbed a foam noodle and helped me move faster. We climbed out of the water. "What's going on, Buddy?"

We followed Buddy to the bow of the boat as he pointed into the water. There were two stingrays gliding through the water near the sandy bottom about where we had been.

"I didn't want you to frighten them. They are usually docile; but if threatened, the barbs on their long tails are deadly poisonous."

"Thank you for letting us know," I said.

Buddy added, "I think it will be safe for us to go to the Thunderball Cave today. It is only about two miles away. I've already talked to Hank and Sarah, and we'll pick them up in our dinghy."

A short while later, we rode to Staniel Cay. Thunderball Cave got its name from the movie Thunderball. Several scenes were shot there. The cave is a limestone formation with an underwater passageway to the grotto. It was windy there, and the current was strong. Being claustrophobic, I knew I would not be able to swim through a small passage underwater without flustering. Buddy dropped the dinghy's anchor to keep from drifting. The men put on their masks, snorkels and fins and hopped into the water. Sarah and I remained on the dinghy.

About 20 minutes later, the guys surfaced and returned to the dinghy. "How was it, Tyler" I asked.

"It was a great experience. The entrance was narrow. Then it opened into an underwater cave. The sun shone through an opening at the top of the grotto. I saw all kinds of tropical fish, too."

Hank added, "I'm glad Buddy knew where the entrance was to the cave. I would not have been able to find it."

Buddy pulled up the anchor, and we headed back to Big Major's Spot. A large yacht had moored. In addition, a local excursion boat was beached with tourists, dotting the shore and feeding the pigs. I was glad we went there yesterday.

As Tyler and I were sitting in the cockpit, we watched a couple return to the yacht on jet skis. They idled to the stern of the boat and slipped onto a hydraulic dock. Once on the stern, the dock raised up flush with the rear of the boat. We waved at them. Not long after that, they lowered a center-consoled Boston Whale into the water and came over to say hello.

"That's a beautiful yacht," I said, "Are you here on vacation?"

The guy replied with an Australian accent, "No, we are crew on that boat. The captain is delivering it to Puerto Rico for its owners to use for a holiday. They are a family from India."

I said, "We are crew as well!" Our captain is taking the catamaran to Georgetown for its owner. My name is Aspen, and this is Tyler."

The girl responded, "I am Clara, and this is Robert."

Tyler asked, "What are your job duties?"

Entrance to Thunderball Grotto, location for a scene from the movie, Thunderball, near Staniel Cay, Exuma

Robert said, "I am the first mate and help the captain, who is also the cook. Clara is the social director. She plans activities for the family while on vacation, watches their children and keeps their living quarters clean."

Noting Tyler's accent, Clara asked, "Tyler, where are you from?"

"England," he replied.

"Would you like to see the inside of the yacht?" Robert asked.

"Of course!' I exclaimed.

They motioned for us to join them on their boat, and we sped over to the yacht. It was 98 feet long. The inside was like a mini-cruise ship. We walked on sheets of brown paper that covered the floors and hallways to keep them clean for the owners. The captain was playing his role as cook in an enormous galley. Clara showed us upstairs where the family lived. Downstairs was the crew quarters. The salon was huge and had a big-screen TV with ample luxurious seating. I was careful not to touch anything. After the tour, they drove us back to our catamaran.

After they left, I said to Tyler, "I thought the catamaran was roomy. It's a lot less space to keep clean."

Over dinner, I asked Buddy, "What is our next destination?"

"Little Farmer's Cay," he replied.

"How far away is that?" questioned Tyler.

"It's about 20 nautical miles. It should take us only a couple of hours to get there," Buddy replied. "We have a good weather window if we leave tomorrow."

CHAPTER 30

Little Farmer's Cay

Hank and Sarah followed us again on our course to Little Farmer's Cay and found a place to moor. The seas were a little choppy with waves about two to three feet. There were a few clouds in the sky but mostly sunny. We entered the inlet, and Buddy selected a suitable mooring buoy. Tyler and I worked together to secure the lines. I grabbed the boat hook and pulled the floating ball close to the port side of the boat. This ball had a polypropylene line pulled through the eye of the buoy. Typically, we tied off to a metal ring. I held the ball while Tyler used the boat hook to slip the line through the polypropylene loop and secure it back to the forward starboard cleat. We did the same thing on the opposite side.

We lowered the dinghy, idled into the harbor and found a spot at the courtesy docks. We followed the walkway up the hill. Seeing a restaurant, we decided to stop for lunch. The owner was very friendly and informative. The island is inhabited by about 60 people, and all of them are related. There is school for the children on the island. Other than fish and garden vegetables, everything else has to be imported. Once a week, a freighter came to port with supplies.

Next to the restaurant was a small shop. I went in to look around. There were several shelves of shell art. I selected one that had delicate flowers made from shells and that were secured to a piece of staghorn coral. I also bought a loaf of homemade bread.

We went back to the dinghy and motored back to the catamaran. Before dinner, Buddy was listening to the local weather on our weather side band radio. There was a front coming in with high winds. Buddy decided we would stay here for a couple of days until the weather cleared up.

Hank and Sarah came for dinner and a movie. During our conversation, we learned that Hank had served on a Merchant Marine ship in his younger days. He learned maintenance and boat repair during his tenure. After the movie, we escorted them to their skiff at the stern of our boat. I watched them return to their boat with their blue string of lights on the mast.

On Thursday morning, I asked Buddy if we could use the glass-bottom kayak. Of course, he agreed. Tyler and I paddled around the area near the boat. The bottom was alive with coral and colorful fish. We saw another catamaran like ours and paddled over to say hello. There were a family of four and their dog onboard. They were from the States and spent the summer in the Bahamas.

Next we rowed to White Beach and pulled the kayak to shore. True to its name, the beach had pristine white sand. We walked to the end of the beach. There was a large, old derelict boat beached on the shore. From the looks of it, the vessel had been there a long time. Walking back toward the kayak, a cargo ship idled into the bay. "I wonder if that is one of the boats that bring supplies to the island?" I asked Tyler.

He replied, "It's possible. Look! They are anchoring."

We watched several boats lowered into the water on the port side with several crew. They were laden with crates. The driver motored to the marina at the yacht club. Several men were waiting for them. They unloaded the supplies. "That is something you don't see every day," I said.

"We should get back to the catamaran. My arms are tired from so much paddling," I added.

We glided past the stern of the supply ship. Tyler said, "It has a Bahamian flag, and the boat's name is Osprey."

Tyler said, "You would think these freighters would be from the United States."

"Who knows?" I responded.

Back at the Hodos, Buddy helped us secure the kayak to the starboard side of the bow. I spent the rest of the day washing and drying clothes and general clean-up around the boat. I also caught up on some reading.

Tyler helped hoist Buddy up the mast to change the light bulb at the top of the mast. While Buddy was up there, he took some photos from 74 feet in the air of the clear water around the boat. Buddy completed his task, and Tyler lowered him back to the deck.

I decided to fix lasagna for dinner. I made garlic bread with the loaf I bought yesterday. Tyler helped me prepare the salad. We sat out in the cockpit and enjoyed a beautiful rainbow that coursed over the radio tower on the island.

Rainbow over island of Little Farmer's Cay, Exuma

CHAPTER 31

Mayday, Mayday!

I woke up in the night by the boat rocking back and forth. It was banging on something. I grabbed my phone. It was 1:30 a.m. I jumped out of bed. "Tyler!" I yelled. "Something is wrong! Wake up!"

Then I ran up the stairs to the salon, turning on a light. It was a mess. A galley drawer was open, with utensils strewn all over the floor and anything else that had not been stowed. I reached the other side of the salon and rapped on Buddy's door. "Wake up, Buddy!"

Buddy immediately opened his door and said, "I think we've hit something! We've got to get to the flybridge!" He scrambled open the cockpit door. Tyler and I were right behind him. It was pitch black, and the wind was blowing.

"I can't see anything! It's too dark!" I cried.

Buddy said, "I can't get my bearings. I don't know where we are! I think we have gone aground! Can anyone see a landmark?"

I searched for Herb's blue lights on his trawler. "Why did he have to cut them off tonight?"

Tyler said, "I see the radio tower lights! They're over there!" He pointed directly behind the boat.

"Buddy, do you hear that alarm? It sounds like it is somewhere on the boat."

"Oh, no!" Buddy replied, "It might be the bilge pump. We're taking on water somewhere!" He ran downstairs, and we followed.

Buddy assessed the situation and said, "We are taking on water in the forward section of the starboard pontoon. But not to worry - the pontoons have separate compartments, and the leak is contained at the tip of the pontoon. The boat won't sink."

"What do we do now?" Tyler asked.

"The mooring lines must have broken free during the wind, and we have drifted over to the rocky side of the bay. I'll go power up the boat, put the engines in reverse and try to get the boat back into the water," Buddy reasoned. "Tyler, get the spotlight from the cockpit locker and bring it up to the flybridge, so I can see better."

I prayed silently. "Dear Lord, please guide us. What can I do to help?" Instantly, the thought came to mind. "I'm going to call for help on the marine radio," I said.

"You can try, but I doubt you'll reach anyone at this hour," Buddy responded.

I called out a mayday and repeated my plea every minute or so. It seemed like forever, but miraculously someone answered my distress call!

"Hello," the voice said. "What's wrong?"

"This is the Hodos. Our mooring line broke loose; and we are grounded, taking on water!"

"Can you make it to the marina?"

I ran up to the flybridge with the portable marine radio. "Buddy, someone answered my distress call! He wants to know if we can make it to the marina?"

"Tell him, yes, we'll try; but it's very windy and will be hard to dock."

I repeated Buddy's words to the man.

He replied, "I'll meet you at the marina docks. I'll bring help. We'll get there before you will."

"Thank you so much!"

Buddy had managed to get the boat afloat. With the powerful spotlight, he navigated across the bay, dodging other moored vessels. By God's grace, we made it to the marina. The wind was blowing away from the marina, making it impossible for us to dock.

Four or five men were standing at the dock. They heaved lines to us, pulled the catamaran to the dock and secured it to the bollards. We all jumped onto the dock. One of the men commented that he saw the hole in the pontoon. Buddy examined the tip of the pontoon as best he could with a flashlight.

An older gentleman approached and said, "My name is John. I spoke to you on the marine radio. I also brought along my wife who is a nurse in case she was needed."

"How did you happen to have your radio on at that hour?" I asked.

He responded, "I couldn't sleep and got up to get a snack. I always keep a VHS radio on because I own the marina."

"Thank You, Jesus! What a blessing You were!" I responded.

Buddy walked over and asked the marina owner, "Do you mind if we stay at your dock overnight? We're not taking on any water. I can survey the damage better in the morning."

"Certainly," John said.

We tried to get some sleep for the rest of what was left of the night.

Buddy was up bright and early Friday morning to survey the damage. There was a hole in the tip of the starboard pontoon from a piece of limestone rock from the shore about the size of a grapefruit. The port hull was scratched up, but there was no hole. God protected us from a major catastrophe.

Buddy discussed our situation with us over coffee in the salon. "If I had just used the alarm system, this wouldn't have happened."

Limestone formation near Big Major's Spot, Exuma

I tried to reassure him, "Buddy, you can't blame yourself."

"I've got some marine putty that will seal underwater. I can make that temporary repair, and we can go back to the anchorage and find another mooring near Hank and Sarah. He has some experience with hull repair. I'll talk to him before I call Harvey," Buddy added. "Tyler, can you help me with the repair?"

"I'll be happy to assist you," he answered.

"Then let's get to work. You get our mask and snorkels, and I'll get the putty."

After several hours of work, Buddy was satisfied that the patch would hold enough for us to move back to the anchorage. Buddy went up to the marina office and informed John that we were leaving.

"How much do I owe you for staying at your dock overnight?"

John replied, "Nothing. You already paid for four days at the mooring. I'm really sorry about what happened."

"Thank you and your family for your assistance last night. We're moving back to the mooring since it's paid for," Buddy said.

We made it back to the anchorage without any problems. Hank and Sarah saw us, got into their skiff and waited for us to moor. "This time, I'm going to swim down and check the lines and the ground tackle to make sure they are secure. I'll use the positional alarm system as well," Buddy said.

When they saw Buddy return to the boat, they motored over to see us. After listening to Buddy's story, Hank said, "I keep a small supply of resin and fiberglass. I'll be happy to close that hole, so you can get to a boatyard that can do the proper repair."

"That is kind of you. How much do you charge for your work?"

"Nothing. You have been so kind to us. It's the least I can do."

Hank continued, "Early in the morning at low tide, beach the catamaran over at White Beach. I can complete the job before the tide rises."

After Hank and Sarah left, Buddy decided to call Harvey on the satellite phone. After the conversation was over, Buddy told us the plan. "If all goes well in the morning, we'll leave for Spanish Wells this Saturday. There are not many boatyards that can pull out a 28-foot-wide boat. Harvey talked to them, and they'll be finished with their current job in a couple of days. He agreed with the temporary repair that Hank will do tomorrow. We'll stop at Warderick Wells and then on to Spanish Wells."

"That means we'll go back through the Yellow Bank and Current Cut again," I spoke.

"Yes, but we're pros now. It won't be a problem," Buddy replied.

CHAPTER 32

Sabotage

Before sunrise, we motored across the harbor to White Beach on Saturday morning. Buddy cut the engines and slowly idled to the shore. Upon beaching the catamaran, he gently revved the engines to secure the forward part of the pontoons well up on the shore. Hank followed in his skiff and beached as well. Buddy had to lower the dinghy. He brought it around to the left front pontoon and wedged the bow under it to allow an unobstructive view of the patched hole. Hank got the resin and fiberglass out of his boat and set it on the ground next to the pontoon.

Hank asked Buddy, "Do you have a small paint brush?"

"I don't think so, but let me look." Buddy returned to the stern and climbed aboard on the swim ladder. He rummaged through the supply locker.

"How's it going?" I asked.

"I'm looking for a small paint brush for Hank. I've found some larger ones but no small ones."

I said, "I have a small paint brush. The lady who does my hair gave me a bottle of hair dye and a small brush to apply it – just in case I needed a touch up." I went to my toiletry bag, retrieved the small fan-shaped bristle brush and gave it to Buddy.

Buddy replied, "It's worth a try. Thanks."

Returning to shore, Buddy showed my small paint brush to Hank. "Will this do?"

"It's perfect!"

Hank, Buddy and Tyler worked together to mix the resin, apply the fiberglass and seal it with the resin. When it had dried sufficiently, Hank smoothed out the edges with a buffer. Other than the gray color of the resin against the white pontoon, it was a perfect job. Buddy thanked Hank profusely. He offered again to pay him.

Hank politely refused, saying he was a Christian. God had given him this talent, he said, and it was his pleasure to help Buddy with the repair.

As soon as the tide was high enough to float the pontoon, Buddy started his engines, put them in reverse and slowly left the beach. We headed back to our new mooring and secured the boat.

Over lunch, Buddy said, "I've been thinking about it. I'm curious as to how the Hodos broke loose from the mooring. I checked the lines we used for mooring on the bow; and I could not find any wear, tear or fraying. Let's take the dinghy to the original spot. I want to dive down and look at the ground tackle and buoy."

I tagged along, and we drove over to the first mooring. Buddy jumped into the water with his mask and snorkel. The water was clear, and we could see him well. Shortly afterward, Buddy surfaced and climbed into the dinghy. "The cement block and chain were secure,"

Buddy said. "Tyler, did you secure to a metal ring?"

"No," Tyler replied. "It was a polypropylene loop."

"I think we were sabotaged. The polypropylene loop was cut. That explains why our lines had no damage. Once the loop was cut, our lines were loose and that is why we drifted."

"Why would anyone cut the mooring loop?" I asked.

"I don't know," replied Buddy. "Let's ride into town to see if anyone witnessed anything strange."

We went to the marina to talk to John. Buddy explained what happened. "Do you have a police station here?"

John remarked, "Of course not! Everybody on the island is related - besides the boaters and tourists."

"There is no crime on the island?"

John replied, "Not among the family. But we did have to contact the police station on Staniel Cay once because a tourist reported something stolen from her room at the Yacht Club. Buddy, why don't you come with me, and we'll talk with the boys who manage the courtesy docks and with Tom who owns the restaurant in town."

"Thank you," Buddy replied.

Tyler and I walked behind John and Buddy. "Aspen, I have a bad feeling about this."

"What do you mean?"

Tyler explained, "This sounds like something my uncle would orchestrate."

I responded, "How could he possibly know our whereabouts? Why would he do something like this?"

Tyler said, "Revenge."

Buddy overheard our conversation, "You think you know who did this, Tyler?"

Tyler told Buddy how we met, found the treasure, that his Uncle Allen had served time in prison, was paroled and recently left England. Tyler concluded as they neared the courtesy dock with John, "My uncle is burdened with resentment because I helped Aspen in her pursuit for her ancestor's inheritance that was stored in a box in his attic. I have no idea how he found us."

John asked the young man at the courtesy dock if he had seen anyone suspicious dock there in the past few days. He had not seen anyone other than the current guests and boaters visiting the island. Then they walked up to the Seaside Restaurant. John talked with Tom and asked if he had seen anyone come in within the past few days that seemed uneasy.

Tom thought for a moment. "It's hard to say. So many people stop here for a good meal. My wife and I try to talk to everyone who visits. We get busy sometimes and can't welcome everyone."

Tyler asked, "Do you recall if any of them are from England?"

"The mailboat service came in yesterday to the island bringing supplies. The captain and some of his crew came for a meal yesterday. I believe a few of them had English accents."

Do you remember if one of them had spectacles, white hair and a beard?" asked Tyler.

Tom said, "There were a couple of white-haired men." He thought for a moment. "I recall one wore glasses."

"Could that be your uncle, Tyler?" I asked.

"It is possible. But why would he be crewing on a ship in the Exumas?"

Buddy asked, "Do you know where the vessel goes from here?" Tom replied, "It's hard to say. They could have gone south to Black Point or north toward Highborne Cay. These boats come from a port in Nassau. Dry goods are imported from the various trade services on the east coast of Florida, and the smaller mailboat services the various island chains."

"Thanks for your help, Tom," John said.

We left the restaurant in a quandary.

Tyler said, "I wonder which island Osprey is going to next."

"It's at least a couple of days ahead of us," Buddy replied. "We'll definitely keep a lookout for them when we leave tomorrow."

On the way back to the Hodos, we stopped by the Eternity and said goodbye to Hank and Sarah. "Thank you, Hank, for the excellent job you did on the hull," Buddy said.

"You are most welcome. Glad I could be of assistance."

"We are headed back to Spanish Wells for a permanent repair," Buddy responded.

Hank said, "We are leaving tomorrow as well. Our next stop is Black Point. If the weather holds, we should get to Georgetown in a couple of days."

Sarah asked, "Before you leave, we would like to pray for you."

Before Buddy could respond, I said, "Of course, we don't mind!"

Hank prayed for safe travelling mercies, that the temporary patch would hold and that we would make it safely to Spanish Wells. Tyler, in turn, prayed for Hank and Sarah's safe passage.

We returned to the Hodos and secured the dinghy for our journey. I emailed my mom and dad with our itinerary. Spanish Wells was the next port with internet. After dinner, we stowed loose items for travel tomorrow. Thus ended another interesting day.

CHAPTER 33

Warderick Wells

Warderick Wells was less than three hours away. The forecast was rain in the evening there. Buddy cautiously idled away from Little Farmer's Cay. Once out in the open sea, we hoisted the main sail and headed northward. The winds were just right for sailing, and the waves were one to two feet. The temporary patch was doing its job. Unfortunately, there was no sign of a mailboat.

Warderick Wells, home to the Exuma Land and Sea Park, is protected by the Bahamas National Trust. We reached the entrance to the channel, the most beautiful area I had seen so far. The anchorage had room for about 20 vessels. They were lined up in a row as we passed them by. They were on each side of the deep channel sandbars in shallow water. Because of the variance in depths, the water looked variegated with varying shades of blue, turquoise and white.

Buddy called ahead to reserve a mooring buoy. Our spot was farther away from the entrance but closest to the guest dinghy dock. As soon as we secured our lines to the mooring ball, it began to rain and the winds picked up. Oddly, the sky had a purplish glow and added to the idyllic beauty of this area.

This was the first storm we had at anchor. After settling in, we ate dinner and watched a movie before going to bed. Buddy set the positional alarm. In my cabin, the constant splashing of the water on the pontoons lulled me to sleep.

The next morning over breakfast, Buddy said, "We weathered the storm fine last night. No problems with the mooring. We didn't take on any water."

"That's a blessing!" I exclaimed.

Buddy added, "The rain has stopped, but it's still windy at about 20 knots. We'll remain here today."

"Is it too windy to go ashore?" Tyler asked.

Buddy replied, "The dinghy will handle the wind. It's a short distance to the courtesy dock. You two go and have some fun. I'm going to hang around the boat."

Looking out the window, I noticed a dinghy circling around the bow of our boat. "What are they doing out there?"

Buddy said, "I'll find out." He ventured out to the bow. Tyler and I saw him conversing with the couple, and then he returned.

"Anything wrong?" I asked.

"You aren't going to believe this. They heard about what happened to us at Little Farmer's and were curious about the repair work."

Tyler said, "I wonder how they found out about it."

Buddy responded, "They had been at Little Farmer's too and had seen us repairing it on the beach."

After another cup of coffee, I was ready to go visit the park. Thankfully, I had a hooded wind jacket that shielded the wind. We lowered the dinghy and putted over to the guest dock.

We met a few other boaters at the park office. They were getting ready to hike to the other side of the park. We asked if they would like us to join them.

Near the park entrance - on the shore facing the anchorage - was the skeleton of a sperm whale. It had beached there and died because it swallowed a plastic bag and suffocated. We followed the path through a jungle of mangroves and other shrubs. We crossed a rocky ledge called the Sunshine Causeway. It wasn't long before we came upon Boo-Boo Hill, the highest point on the island. Here boaters have made their mark by writing the name of their vessel, their names and year they visited the park in a huge pile of wooden planks.

The view from the hill was beautiful. We could see the anchorage on one side and the open ocean's waves crashing against the rocks on the other side. The shoreline was jagged with limestone formations. After taking some pictures, we returned by the same trail.

Back at the park office, the manager said that, on the weekends, the staff had a cookout on the beach. Everyone was invited to attend. He asked if we had any questions about the island.

Tyler asked, "How do you get your supplies that stock your store?"

He replied, "We get our supplies from a mailboat service from Nassau. In fact, they were just here yesterday."

"Do you know where they are going next?" Tyler questioned.

"Highborne Cay is their next stop. I think they go to Spanish Wells before they return to Nassau. If you don't mind me asking, why do you want to know?"

Tyler replied, "I am looking for my uncle. I think he is aboard the Osprey."

The park ranger replied, "That's the ship! I hope you can catch up with them."

We returned to the catamaran to find Buddy napping in the salon. We tried to walk in quietly, but he awoke.

"Sorry, Buddy," I said. "We didn't mean to wake you."

"That's alright. I need to get up anyway. Did you have fun?"

Tyler said, "Other than the wind, we had a nice hike to Boo-Boo Hill and back." He added, "I talked to the park ranger. The Osprey was here yesterday, and the next stop is Highborne Cay. After there, they either return to Nassau or make one more stop at Spanish Wells."

Buddy replied, "Seems we are a day behind them. If the weather and seas are favorable, we can make it to Spanish Wells tomorrow."

"The staff at the park office is going to have a cookout on the beach tonight. Do you think we could attend?" I asked.

Buddy replied, "Of course! Can I join you?"

"Certainly!" Tyler responded.

"What time do we need to be there?"

I said, "The other boaters are gathering about 6 p.m."

"Do we need to bring anything?" Buddy queried.

"They supply the hot dogs, hamburgers and chips. All we need to bring is our drinks."

Buddy added, "I'll get cleaned up and will be ready when you are."

The wind was still blowing at about 20 knots that night. Someone made a bonfire on the beach near the picnic tables and a permanent grill. We chatted with other boaters. Some we had met before on other islands. It was dark when the group broke up. All the boaters had their dinghies at the dock. The dock had lights, so we had little trouble reaching our dinghy. Buddy brought a large flashlight that we used to ride back to the Hodos.

We were all glad to return to the warmth of the boat and sat down in the salon. Buddy said, "I plan to leave in the morning for Spanish Wells. We'll see how the sea conditions are when we leave the anchorage."

"I know you're anxious to get the hull permanently repaired," I remarked.

Buddy replied, "Harvey is anxious as well."

Tyler and Buddy continued the conversation. I showered and got ready for bed. Tomorrow probably will be a long day.

CHAPTER 34

Allen's Cay Revisited

This morning, we left Warderick Wells. Every island has its own unique features. I will miss the breathtaking anchorage here. We idled through the narrow channel past the other sailboats. The open water proved to be very rough. Buddy decided to move closer to the shoreline of the islands, and we stopped at Allen's Cay again.

Buddy lowered the dinghy and went to the bow of the boat to inspect the viability of the temporary patch. He noticed a tiny patch on the hull. He thought it might be a benign air bubble. Buddy returned to the stern. Tyler and I were relaxing in the cockpit. Buddy said, "One of the sailboats from Warderick Wells just came into the inlet. I'm going to see if he needs any help."

We acknowledged his statement and waved to him. Tyler said, "Isn't that the gent who got into an argument with his crew at the cookout?"

"Yes, I think so," I answered. "He looks to be by himself."

"I wonder what happened?" Tyler asked.

"Maybe Buddy will find out and tell us when he comes back," I replied.

Buddy returned about an hour later. "How did it go?" I asked.

Buddy said, "Charley was alone. I helped him anchor."

"So his crew really abandoned him?" I asked.

"I can't fathom sailing a large boat alone," Tyler said.

Buddy explained, "Charley posted a classified advertisement on a website for finding crew. He hired Andy from this listing, but they did not get along. One thing led to another, and Andy told Charley he was leaving. Charley didn't believe him until this morning when he woke up. Andy wasn't there, and his belongings were gone. Charley thinks he wants to get a job at the Land and Sea Park."

I asked, "What is he going to do?"

"He's going back to Florida. He said he's getting too old to sail alone," Buddy said.

"I feel sorry for the chap," Tyler remarked.

"He's an experienced sailor; he should have no problem crossing over from Nassau in good weather," Buddy added. "Charley did tell me about some friends of his who live in Spanish Wells. He gave me their number and told me to call them, and they would help us when we get there."

"Tomorrow is going to be a good day," Buddy said. "The weather forecast is clear and sunny. Next stop - Spanish Wells!"

CHAPTER 35

Spanish Wells

We waited until mid-morning to sail out on Tuesday. Buddy wanted the sun to be overhead through our trip through the Yellow Bank. Tyler and I kept watch for the black shadows of coral. Buddy slowly powered through the maze. Once clear from that area, we hoisted the sails and made good time to Current Cut. We lowered the mainsail, and Buddy powered through the channel - again with no problem.

We made it to Spanish Wells about an hour later. This time we were docking at the only marina in the port. Buddy called ahead on the VHS marine radio and secured the reservation. The slips were large and covered as well. Having phone reception here, Buddy contacted Charley's friends Larry and Marge. They met us at the marina in their golf cart. We introduced ourselves, and they took us back to their home.

Marge served us refreshments, and we admired their bungalow.

"How long have you lived here?" I asked.

"We retired about 10 years ago, sold our home in the States and moved here, "Marge explained.

Larry added, "We love the people and the weather here. Charley told us that you are getting your boat repaired."

"Yes," Buddy remarked.

"Where will you stay while it is in the boatyard?" Marge asked.

"I think we'll be able to stay on the boat while it is being repaired."

Larry said, "I'd like to show you around town. We can take the golf cart."

We thanked Marge for the snacks. Buddy sat up front with Larry and Tyler, and I sat in the back. He showed us the grocery store, gift shops, the marine supply store, the three churches in town and a hardware store - to name a few. I learned that the grocery store was a co-op, which means that the people who shop there own the store. These members make the decisions of what items to stock on the shelves.

Larry took us back to the R&B Boatyard. He introduced us to Bob, the owner of the business. Bob explained to Buddy that Harvey had contacted him concerning the repair and payment of the pontoon.

"We have a slip at the marina. Do you know when you can haul our boat out?' Buddy questioned.

Bob replied, "You can bring her around 9 a.m. Thursday."

Larry added, "Buddy, you can use my golf cart during your stay."

Buddy said, "That's generous of you. Won't you need it to get around town?"

"Everything is within walking distance here. I need the exercise!" Larry replied.

"Bless you!" I exclaimed.

Larry left Buddy the keys and strolled down the street.

We took the cart back to the marina and left it in the parking lot at the entrance to the ramp. We walked back to the boat and got ready for dinner. The sunset was beautiful, looking west from the harbor.

CHAPTER 36

Lobster Tails

Tyler and I had a day to wander around Spanish Wells. Buddy took the golf cart to the hardware store. We decided to walk into town. There were only two streets to cross to reach the grocery store. When we reached the parking lot, I spotted a boutique.

"Let's see what's in that souvenir shop over there," I said to Tyler.

As we stepped through the door, a bell rang. A lady greeted us. She was well-tanned and wore a yellow frock that accented her blonde hair.

"Hello, welcome to my shop. My name is Debbie. Where are you from?"

"I'm from Georgia, and my boyfriend is from England," I answered.

"What part of Georgia?"

"I'm from Gainesville in the northeast part of the state."

Debbie replied, "I'm from Georgia as well. I grew up in Clarkesville."

"What a small world," Tyler added.

"How did you get to Spanish Wells?" I queried.

"I was visiting here one summer and met a local man. We had a lot in common, and we kept up the rest of the year. I returned again the following summer, and we were married."

"How romantic," I spoke.

"Where are you staying?" asked Debbie.

"We are in a catamaran at the marina dock," I replied.

We looked around the shop. Tyler spied conch shells that were fashioned to blow like a horn. "I've always wanted one of these. May I give it a go?"

"Certainly," replied Debbie.

Tyler put the drilled opening at the end of the shell, took a deep

Spanish Wells Beach, Eleuthera

breath and blew. It produced a musical sound like a trumpet.

"I'll take it," Tyler said and made his purchase.

I found a pair of earrings and a matching necklace. "I'd like this set," I said as I brought them to the register.

"Thank you. I made them," Debbie replied.

"That makes the set even more special. You are so talented."

"Thank you!"

As we were leaving, Debbie asked, "Do you like lobster tails?"

"We love them. I've read that a lot of people here catch lobster for a living," I said.

"Yes, it is my husband and his family's occupation. I have some lobster tails in the freezer if you would like them."

I replied, "Thank you very much, but I don't cook much. It was very nice to meet a fellow Georgian."

"Me, too," she replied.

"Debbie was very nice," Tyler said.

"Yes, she was. Everybody I've met here has been friendly."

We walked to the grocery store and picked up a few items. We walked to the white sand beach. The tide was out, extending the area between the beautiful turquoise water. We crossed over a bridge. I took a picture of a small boat anchored in a thin channel of water between the sandbar and the beach. It was a peaceful scene.

We walked leisurely back to the marina. The golf cart was back, indicating Buddy was probably on the boat. We saw Buddy talking to a couple on a sailboat that had pulled into a slip beside us. We walked over to say hello.

Buddy saw us and said to us, "Do you remember these folks? Barb and Jim were anchored near us on Royal Island about a week ago."

I thought for a moment. "I remember their boat was anchored on the other side of Hank and Sarah."

Buddy said, "They invited us over for appetizers before dinner."

"We'll bring chips and salsa," I said. Tyler and I had picked that up at the grocery store.

Barb said, "I've got vegetables and dip. We'll be ready about 5 o'clock."

We all returned to the boat. I put up the rest of the groceries. Tyler made a jug of tea and found some cups. By the time we had showered and changed, it was time to visit Jim and Barb.

They had a 36-foot sailboat with a center cockpit. There were two benches on either side of the cockpit. Barb had placed a table in the center for us to share our snacks. While we were socializing, Barb said to me, "There is someone over there at your boat."

I looked up and recognized Debbie. "Debbie, we're over here," I shouted.

She responded by walking over to where we were. Debbie was carrying something that smelled delicious. "Hi, Aspen." She handed to me an aluminum container with 12 baked lobster tails - still hot from the oven.

"Thank you very much! You didn't have to go to all that trouble."

She replied, "No trouble at all. Georgia girls stick together. Consider it Southern hospitality! Sorry I can't stay longer, but my husband is coming back from his catch of lobsters today."

She left as quickly as she came. Barb said, "How did you know her?"

"Tyler and I just met her today. She owns the gift shop next to the grocery store. She and I are both from Georgia, and our hometowns are about an hour apart."

Tyler added, "Her husband owns a couple of lobster boats." Barb and Jim were in shock that we shared our feast with them. The appetizers turned into a meal for us. They were leaving tomorrow for the Abaco Islands.

"I will pray for fair winds and following seas," I said as we left their vessel and settled back in the Hodos for the night.

CHAPTER 37

Repair Day

The next morning, Tyler and Buddy left the marina and idled a short way to the R&B Boatyard. Buddy asked me to drive the golf cart to the shop. I got to the dock before they did. I parked the vehicle and walked onto the dock. Bob and several workers were waiting for the Hodos at the slip. Bob walked down the dock, so Buddy could hear his instructions. "We'll be hauling your catamaran by means of a syncrolift. Idle your boat into the slip, and then cut the engines. There is a cradle just under the water. For safety reasons, all of you and your crew will need to get off the boat. Once you are on the dock, then we will attach some pulleys, perform a synchronized hoist, lift the cradle up out of the water and flush the dock. We will secure the pontoons with supports. We won't begin work until you get what you need off the boat."

"Where are we going to stay, Buddy?" I asked.

"I have a surprise or, should I say, Harvey has a surprise. He has made reservations for us to stay at the guest house at the marina."

"That's why you asked me to bring the golf cart!"

"Bob placed a ladder for easy access on the boat. Come around and pack a bag," Buddy stated.

We loaded the cart with our belongings and drove back to the marina. Our accommodations included two separate rooms. There were two queen-size beds in one room, where Tyler and Buddy would sleep, and a convertible sofa in the living area and kitchen. There also were Wi-Fi and cable TV. All the rooms and the restaurant overlooked the harbor.

Once settled in our room, Tyler and I got our laptop computers and sat at the kitchen table. Buddy sat on the couch, flipping through endless TV channels.

We both checked our emails. As I was sending a reply to my mother, Tyler said, "OH, no!"

"What's wrong?"

Hodos at gas dock in Spanish Wells, Eleuthera

"I got an email from Hilda. She says that Uncle Allen is gone!"

"When is the date of the email?" I asked, knowing we had not had internet since the first time we were at Spanish Wells almost two weeks ago.

"She sent it last Monday. I think we were at Big Major's Spot."

"What does she say?" I questioned.

Tyler read, "About a week ago, I received a visit from a constable and Allen's parole officer, Mr. Timmons. Mr. Timmons said that Allen had weekly appointments with him; and this week, he did not appear for his meeting. He asked me if I knew of his whereabouts. I told them that I knew nothing.

"They asked me if I would take them to Allen's house since I had a key. Of course, I complied. They searched his study and confiscated his laptop. Today Mr. Timmons called me. Allen's laptop history had been searched and revealed that he boarded a freighter bound for Florida. I just thought you needed to know."

Tyler said, "I am trying to piece things together. Somehow Uncle Allen was able to obtain passage on a cargo ship returning to Florida. Somehow he makes it to the Bahamas and ends up on a mailboat service. The odds of us being on Little Farmer's Cay simultaneously must be a coincidence."

Buddy had been listening to our conversation and said, "I haven't seen the mailboat here. Someone in Spanish Wells should know when and where it will be anchored. I'm going to check with Bob."

Tyler said, "I'll go with you."

I took that advantage to take a shower and wash my hair.

A short time later, Buddy and Tyler came back to the apartment. "What did you find out?" I queried.

"The Osprey comes in tomorrow. It anchors at the harbor entrance. They will lower their skiffs, go to the fuel docks and tie off. The boatyard and the small grocery store - just down from the gas docks - are expecting deliveries. Guess where the captain and crew come for dinner," Buddy said.

"The dockside marina restaurant?" I asked. "Yes!" Tyler exclaimed.

CHAPTER 38

The Plan

On Friday morning at breakfast, Buddy said, "Let's talk about our plans for today. Bob said the ship arrives around noon, anchors, unloads the supplies and delivers them to us and the grocery store next door. We can take the golf cart and park where we can watch who delivers the goods, or we can walk down the street and find a strategic place to notice the activity."

"Why don't we go this morning and see which option is best?" I asked.

Tyler added, "We left the dinghy in the slip, so one of us could take a ride and observe them unload the cargo."

Buddy said, "I think I should do that since Allen doesn't know me. Tyler, do you have a picture of him?"

Tyler flipped through the pictures on his cell phone and found a picture of him and Allen. "This was taken before Allen went to jail, but his features probably haven't changed much."

Buddy looked at the picture. He appeared to have the features Tyler had described to Tom at Little Farmer's Cay. "Could you send this picture to my phone?"

"Sure," Tyler replied.

Then we drove down South Street. There was a restaurant close to the boatyard. The gas docks were in front of the grocery store. We could see several areas where we could park the golf cart.

"Tyler, if Allen delivers the supplies, he will see the Hodos at the boat yard," Buddy said.

"Maybe he never saw the name of the boat. He would have seen the stern, and the name is on each side of the pontoons," Tyler replied.

I added, "There are a lot of catamarans in the area. They all look alike to me."

"He won't be expecting to run into us here," Tyler added.

We returned to the room and developed our plan. Buddy will go for a ride in the dinghy. Tyler and I will wear floppy hats and sunglasses. I will sit at a park bench at the gas docks, and Tyler will stay in the golf cart at the boat yard "parking lot." We will communicate with walkie talkies.

We decided to sit by the pool. We watched ships at a distance at sea. It wasn't long before Buddy saw the mailboat turn toward the harbor through his binoculars. "It's time for me to go take a ride on the dinghy. I'll call you after they have anchored and unloaded their cargo." Tyler and I anxiously waited and watched Buddy's movement.

Forty-five minutes later, Buddy called Tyler, "Crew One and Two, get ready to take your posts."

We jumped up and quickly walked to the golf cart. Tyler parked, and

I walked to the bench as planned. I called Buddy when I was in position. "This is Crew One. I'm at my station." I had Tyler in sight at his post. He gave me a thumbs up.

Buddy responded, "Aye, aye."

I played a game on my phone to pass time. Soon Buddy signaled, "Crew One and Two, the skiffs are loaded and motoring in."

"Roger," I returned.

The two delivery boats idled in and docked close to where I was sitting. One dockworker stayed on each boat, while the other entered the grocery store and the boatyard building. The man came out with an employee and proceeded to the boat. Two hand trucks were produced, and they loaded the boxes and returned to the store. Allen was not one of the workers. A few minutes later, the other crewman returned from the boatyard business office with a worker. They carried several boxes from the second skiff and delivered them to the boatyard.

"The person of interest is not on either boat," I radioed Buddy. "I'm going to the grocery store and buy a snack." I entered the establishment and pretended to shop and browse. The men were unloading the boxes of dry goods. The employee and the dockworker were talking just down the aisle from me. I heard the man from the skiff say, "You won't believe what happened at Little Farmer's Cay." I turned on the voice recorder on my phone and pretended to look for something in the shelves on that aisle.

The employee questioned, "Tell me, Albert!"

Albert continued, "The captain needed a material handler and a hired a man from England when we were docked in Nassau. He was an older gentleman and kept to himself. I asked if he wanted to play poker one night. He joined in and won some money. We played cards frequently, and we became friends. He also made friends with the captain and some other staff. He accompanied them when they went to shore for dinner.

"Allen stays on the boat while we make deliveries. He oversees the inventory and its distribution. When we returned from making deliveries at Little Farmer's Cay, Allen seemed very anxious. After the poker game that night, we went out on the deck. He approached me with a proposition. He told me he would pay me $1,000 if I would do a job for him.

"He asked me to take him in one of the skiffs after midnight to a boat in the anchorage. I needed the money, and I agreed. He asked me to quietly idle to the bow of the boat. He produced a waterproof flashlight and told me to pull up the line on the mooring and cut the loop that secured the line to the bow of the boat. Then he threatened me with bodily harm if I told anyone. We went back to the mailboat. I have avoided him ever since. Please don't tell anybody, Lonnie."

Lonnie said, "I won't. Do you know what happened to the boat?"

"No, we left before sunrise."

While they were still unloading their dry goods, I walked to the cash register, made my purchase and ended the recording. I left the store as calmly as possible, walked quickly to the golf cart and sat down next to Tyler. "Let's get back to the bungalow. I have something you need to hear. I secretly recorded a conversation about Allen at the grocery store."

Tyler hailed Buddy, "This is the Crew Two. Meet us back at the guest house. Mission accomplished."

CHAPTER 39

Reunion

Back at the room, Buddy and Tyler listened to my phone recording of the conversation between Albert and Lonnie. "Good job, Aspen!" Buddy exclaimed. "Spanish Wells has a police station. Let's ride over there with Albert's confession."

Once at the police station, we met with Constable Williams. Tyler recounted Allen's offense that led to his incarceration in England. Then I played the voice recording.

Buddy added, "We think the captain and crew, including Allen, will have dinner at the marina restaurant tonight. We're going there as well."

"I'll confront him," Tyler said. "He will probably try to run. We would like your assistance."

Constable Williams called his detective to our meeting and briefed him on our proposal. He introduced us to Tony Dean. "Tony, I want you to meet the people at their accommodations at the harbor guest house. Be sure to dress in casual attire. Have dinner with them. If there is a problem, don't hesitate to apprehend Allen Dent and bring him to the office for questioning."

Buddy explained, 'Tony, meet us at our place at five o'clock. That would afford us plenty of time to select a suitable table to observe patrons entering the restaurant."

We left the police station and returned to our lodging. "Tyler, this reminds me of our adventure in Allen's attic when we found my ancestor's inheritance."

Tyler said, "I pray that the situation doesn't get chaotic at the restaurant tonight. I'm glad the detective will be joining us."

Buddy said, "We better start getting ready now. We all probably need a shower after today's antics."

Since there was only one bathroom, it took extra time for all of us to clean up. Once prepared for the evening, we gathered in the kitchen and discussed our plan.

Tyler said, "Hopefully, we will be settled at our table eating dinner before the blokes from the Osprey arrive. If Allen doesn't spot us first, once they are feasting, I will approach their table."

"What are you going to say to him?" I asked.

"I'll figure that out when I see his reaction to me. I don't think he is aware that we know about his dirty deed."

There was a knock at the door. It was Tony Dean.

"We're ready to go," Buddy said.

Approaching the marina restaurant, Tyler explained his plans to Tony. "I'll be ready to act - if necessary," Tony replied.

We selected a table for four toward the rear of the restaurant, affording the best view of the room and its occupants. The waitress provided menus.

Buddy said, "Since we're going to be here awhile, let's get an appetizer first."

Tyler ordered crab cakes, and I selected a shrimp cocktail. Buddy and Tony split a seafood appetizer sampler, consisting of oysters, scallops, clams and shrimp.

Then we perused the entrée section. I ordered baked lobster tails. I figured I would not be in Spanish Wells again, so I wanted to enjoy fresh seafood. Tyler selected shrimp scampi. Buddy and Tony had similar tastes - fried anything. They decided on fried shrimp, hush puppies and salad. Buddy returned thanks to the Lord for our meal.

Unfortunately, since we had not seen the Osprey crew yet, we ordered dessert. Each of us ordered types of freshly made pie – key lime, chocolate cream, lemon meringue and banana cream pies. We placed them in the middle of the table, the waitress brought four plates. We shared the huge slices four ways. Then six men entered the dining room. The hostess escorted them to a large table in the middle of the room. Not wanting to be noticeable, Tyler grabbed the dessert menu and peeked over it. He whispered, "I see Uncle Allen. He looks about the same as he did the last time we saw him, Aspen."

The men were oblivious to others in the room as they viewed the menu. Allen sat on the side of the table with his back to us.

"What now?" I asked. "Are you going to speak to him now or wait?"

Buddy suggested, "Let's enjoy our dessert first. They're not going anywhere."

We ordered coffee after we finished our sweets. Now the gentlemen were eating their meals. Tyler said, "I guess it's now or never." He stood up and crossed the dining room to their table. I remained facing away from that direction. The view of the men for Buddy and Tony was un-encumbered.

"What's going on?" I whispered.

Buddy replied, "Tyler approached the men and tapped Allen on the shoulder. Allen turned around and looked up at Tyler. They seem to be exchanging pleasantries. Allen is introducing him to his cohorts. Tyler is whispering something to Allen. Tyler is pointing to our table. Now they are shaking hands. He's coming back to us."

Tyler sat down and took a sip of coffee. "That was tough. I acted surprised to see him. I think he truly was shocked to see me. He introduced me to the men as his nephew. I whispered to Allen that I assumed he was still in England. I asked him to join us when he finished his dinner."

"Do you think he will do that?" I asked.

Tyler said, "It depends. If he thinks we are clueless, he will connect with us. On the other hand, if he thinks we are on to him, he will make a run for it."

We finished our coffee, paid our bill and lingered. The seamen were finishing their meal and rose from their chairs to leave. Allen spoke to one of the men and came over to our table. He pulled up a chair and sat at the end of the table. "Good evening, Aspen."

I said nothing.

Tyler introduced him to Buddy and Tony.

Tyler said, "What a coincidence meeting in Spanish Wells at the same time. Why are you here?"

"I have always wanted to travel to the States. A buddy of mine was a crewman on a freighter. The captain was hiring more workers. I thought it was a good idea to get paid working on a freighter to see the world. That idea was squelched when I realized that the ship traveled back and forth from Florida to England.

"I searched for employment with other boats at the port. I found another cargo ship ready to embark to the Bahamas. Their captain lost his cook, and I took that position. That vessel stopped at Nassau and unloaded some of the crates onto the mailboat that delivered imported goods to various islands. This mailboat cruised to the upper Exuma Islands and Eleuthera. I got a job as a material handler. I oversee the dispersal and inventory of the dry goods. Tomorrow we leave for Nassau to restock for our next delivery.

"How did you and Aspen arrive here?"

Tyler explained, "Aspen and I were hired by a gentleman to be his crew with Buddy to transfer his boat to Georgetown. Tony resides in Spanish Wells, and he is a friend of Buddy's. Unfortunately, the catamaran is here for repair."

At that time, Tony spilled coffee down the front of his shirt. He excused himself to the restroom.

"What happened?" Allen queried.

Buddy answered, "We were moored at Little Farmer's Cay. The second night we were there, we awoke sometime after midnight and our boat was aground with a hole in the pontoon from the rocky shore. We originally thought our lines frayed and slipped though the mooring buoy metal ring.

"Upon inspection the next morning, our mooring lines looked fine. I dove down to check the mooring tackle. Instead of a metal ring attached to the floating buoy, it was a polypropylene loop that had been neatly cut in half by some low-life scum!"

"How do you know that?" Allen queried.

Tyler said, "We didn't know for sure until today."

After looking at me, I handed Tyler my phone. "Listen to this recording."

Tyler turned on the voice recording. As soon as Allen heard Albert's voice, he bolted for the door. Tyler and Buddy ran after him. Allen didn't expect to encounter Tony blocking the door. Buddy tackled Allen to the floor, and Tony handcuffed him and said to us, "I have a nice room where Allen can stay overnight. In the morning, we will perform an interrogation. Please come to the station around 9 a.m., so we can obtain your statements."

CHAPTER 40

The Confession

On Saturday morning, we rode to the police station. The office was small. We sat in the lobby, and Constable Williams offered us coffee. Tony greeted us. He said the Osprey was detained from leaving the harbor until the investigation was completed. The captain, Mr. Jones and Albert appeared shortly after we arrived.

Albert was a slender, young man. His nervousness was manifested by his crossed legs shaking. He kept looking at the captain who tried to console him. "Just tell the truth, Albert."

Buddy was called in for interrogation first. Tyler was next. Shortly after Tyler reported back to the lobby, Tony escorted me to the small room. It only had a table and two chairs opposite each other. "Tell me what happened at the grocery store, Aspen."

I recounted the incident to him. "Please send a copy of the recording to my cell phone." He gave me his number, and I shared the voice recording. "Now all you must do is write a statement of the occurrence and sign it. Then I will accompany you to rejoin the rest of your friends."

Once in the lobby, I said, "I guess you both had to write a testimonial."

Buddy replied, "I documented the evidence of sabotage on the mooring buoy."

"I had to write about Allen's criminal history," Tyler added.

Tony asked for Albert to come in for questioning. He appeared scared and nervous.

The captain was the final witness called by Tony. "I guess he will recall his opinion of Allen," Tyler said.

Constable Williams entered the room after the captain returned. "Thank you all for coming in today. Tony will talk with Allen soon. You all are dismissed for now. Remain in town in case I need to recall anyone."

We returned to our suite. "I'm glad that's over," I said.

Tyler replied, "For the time being."

Buddy said, "I'm going to ride over to the boatyard and see how the repairs are coming along."

Tyler and I took that opportunity to relax by the pool. "Can you believe it has been five weeks since we left St. Marys?"

"I lost track of time. I'm thankful Buddy hired me. I've enjoyed being with you," Tyler answered, squeezing my hand.

I added, "I'm going to miss my crewing experience, but I will carry these memories when I return to school in the fall."

We were still lounging by the pool when Buddy returned from the repair shop. He pulled up a chair and said, "Bob said they should be finished by the first of next week. They're doing a wonderful job."

"Does that mean we will be able to sail to Georgetown?" I asked.

"I'm not sure. I'm going to call Harvey this evening with the update on the restoration."

While we were talking, Tony approached the poolside.

Buddy said, "Hi, Tony. Any news?"

"After interviewing Allen, Constable Williams is arranging for him to be extradited."

Tyler asked, "Will he go to trial?"

"No, he confessed to the sabotage and coercing Albert to cut the line."

"That's shocking! What will happen to Albert?" I asked.

Tony replied, "He will do some service work for the community. The Osprey's captain thinks highly of him. He said he would hold his job until he serves his civic duty."

"Why did my Uncle Allen confess?" Tyler asked.

Tony replied, "That's why I'm here. Allen wants to talk to you and Aspen. I'm here to accompany you. I'll give you time to freshen up and change clothes."

We arrived at the police station with Tony who brought us to a small room with several chairs and a table. Several minutes later, another officer escorted the handcuffed Allen to one of the seats across from us. Tony remained in the room, standing by the door.

"Hello, Uncle," Tyler said, "Tony says you want to talk to us."

Allen cleared his throat and said, "Yes, I do. While I have been incarcerated here, I made friends with a trustee named Jim."

"What is a trustee?" I asked.

Tony answered, "Jim is an inmate who is trustworthy. He performs the duties of a janitor in the police station."

Allen explained, "Each day when Jim is mopping the floors, he stops and talks with me. One day, he shared with me his testimony. He was arrested for shoplifting food because he was jobless and hungry. He felt guilty about his crime. His brother was a churchgoer and asked his pastor to visit Jim."

He continued, "The pastor read to him John 3:16: 'For this is how God loved the world: He gave his one and only Son, so that everyone who believes in him will not perish but have eternal life.' He told Jim about the love of Jesus and said that if he repented of his sin, believed that Jesus died for his sin and committed to change his life, that he would have eternal life.

"Jim gave me a Bible. I told him about all the bad things I have done - the gambling, my selfishness, my anger, my love of money, my assault on you and Aspen; the list goes on.

"Tyler, I never shared your faith and never attended church. But now, I am truly sorry for all the wrongdoings that I have committed against you two. I have asked for forgiveness and prayed with Jim to ask Jesus into my heart to save me. I am asking you earnestly, will you please forgive me?" Allen appealed to Tyler and Aspen.

Tyler and I looked at each other. "Yes, Uncle, I forgive you."

Allen waited for my response. I thought to myself that he seemed sincere and that his demeanor had softened. He even had tears in his eyes. Being a believer in Christ, I knew if Jesus would forgive him, then so could I. "Yes, Allen. I forgive you, too."

"Tony, could you remove these handcuffs please?" Allen requested.

Tony obliged. Allen rose from his chair, raised his arms and asked us to stand. He hugged us. "Thank you, thank you!"

He then held out his hands to Tony who recuffed him.

"Tony will be flying with me to England on Monday. Before I leave, Albert has agreed to see me. I hope he is forgiving as well. When I return to prison, I hope to become a trustee like Jim and share my story with other prisoners. Goodbye for now." The other officer came in and took Allen away.

Tony drove us back to our temporary home. "Thank you, Tony, for all you have done," Tyler said.

"Your uncle certainly had an impact on me," Tony replied. "I go to the Methodist church in town. Would you like to attend the 11 o'clock service tomorrow?"

"We would love to meet you there," I responded.

"Great! See you Sunday," Tony said.

After Tony drove away, we walked back to our room. Buddy was waiting for us in the kitchen. "How did it go?

"You are not going to believe this!" Then Tony and I recounted Allen's story.

"Wow! I didn't see that coming!" Buddy exclaimed. "Praise the Lord!" He added, "Speaking of good news, I talked with Harvey. Due to the circumstances of the damage to the Hodos, his insurance company is going to cover the expenses for the repairs!"

"We have a lot to be thankful for," Tyler said.

CHAPTER 41

Conversion

It was another beautiful day in Spanish Wells. Buddy wanted to come with us to the church. When we arrived, Tony was out in front, waiting for us with Allen. "Thanks for visiting our church," said Tony.

We followed him to an empty pew, and we all sat together. Tyler sat next to Allen. "Well, Uncle, this time we have been seated in church together."

"Yes, I don't know when I will be able to go to church again."

"You should check with the prison chaplain. There might be a Bible study or Sunday service in prison," Tyler suggested.

"Shh," I said. "I think the service is about to begin."

At the close of the service, the pastor offered an altar call.

To our surprise, Allen went down the aisle and kneeled at the altar in prayer. Then he arose, spoke quietly with the pastor and then sat on the front bench.

When the music was over, the pastor called Allen to stand with him. "This is Allen Dent. He has prayed to be saved, and he acknowledges Jesus Christ as his Savior. He is returning to England tomorrow and wishes to be baptized tonight at our evening service." The congregation clapped for joy.

After the service, we all had lunch together at a restaurant near the church. We talked about Allen's conversion and the positive change in him. Tony drove him back to the police station after our meal.

"I hope you will come back to the evening service," Allen said.

"We wouldn't miss it, Uncle!"

No sooner had we returned to the guest house that it seemed it was time to return to the evening service. Allen was baptized at the beginning of the service. During the first hymn, he came back in the sanctuary and sat with us. At the close of the service, many of the church members came to congratulate him.

While walking to the parking lot, Allen said, "I have never felt so loved in my life! Complete strangers hugged me and called me their brother in Christ!"

"We are very happy for you, Allen," Buddy replied. "I pray that you continue to grow in the Lord during your prison term."

Aspen said, "Allen, I have a gift for you." I handed him a gift bag.

He opened the gift and examined a men's devotional book. "Thank you, Aspen. This means a lot to me. I will read it every day along with the Bible given to me by Jim."

Tony was ready to leave, and we saw Allen for the last time before he and Tony left for England. Tyler gave him his address in Atlanta. "Write to me when you have time."

"I will. Farewell!" Allen said as they rode out of the parking lot.

CHAPTER 42

Last Day on Eleuthera

We returned to our suite. There was sandwich meat left in the refrigerator, so I made sandwiches and grabbed a bag of tortilla chips and salsa. While we were cleaning up, Harvey called Buddy. "Hello Harvey, I was going to call you tonight."

"Tyler, let's go sit out on the porch," I said. I did not want to disturb their conversation. We discussed today's wonderful events.

Tyler said, "I wonder what the future holds for us."

"Do you mean continuing to Georgetown after the Hodos is fixed?"

"Well, that, too; but I meant us." Tyler continued, "Aspen, I love you!"

I was astonished. We had been good friends for almost two years and weathered a lot of storms together. I love Tyler, too; but I was insecure about telling him. "I love you, too. I just didn't think you felt the same way." He leaned over from his chair and kissed me.

The moment ended when Buddy opened the door, pulled up a chair and said, "I have some news. Harvey talked to Bob today. The Hodos will be ready tomorrow. Harvey changed his mind. He and his wife are coming to Spanish Wells on Tuesday for her retirement surprise."

Buddy continued, "We'll bring the boat back to the marina. We have a lot of work to do tomorrow. Harvey is paying the airfare for the flight back to Atlanta tomorrow afternoon."

"What are you going to do, Buddy?" I asked.

"Harvey has asked me to continue as captain for a few weeks until he and his wife are comfortable handling the boat."

Tyler said, "I think we all should turn in early and get a good night's sleep. Tomorrow is going to be very busy."

I was so excited; I couldn't fall asleep. So much had happened in the past few days. Day after tomorrow, we will be going home. Tyler will return to work, and I will probably go home and stay at home with my parents until school starts in September. I hoped Tyler and I would have some time to talk on the plane.

Bright and early Monday morning, we drove over to the boatyard. I could not tell that the boat's pontoon had ever been damaged. It looked like new. Buddy said to Bob, "I think Harvey will be pleased with the repair."

"Thank you," Bob replied. "We are very serious about our business." He added, "By the way, Larry said you could leave his golf cart here. I'll drive it over to him after work."

"Please tell him thank you for us. It was such a blessing," replied Buddy.

We watched as they lowered the boat lift into the water. Several employees handled the lines and positioned it next to the dock, allowing us to easily board it. Buddy idled the Hodos back to the slip at the marina, and Tyler and I tied it off to the cleats.

Buddy said, "We won't have to wash the outside of the boat. The folks at R&B Boatyard took care of that for us."

"They even waxed the hulls!" exclaimed Tyler. "She looks like a new catamaran!"

Tyler and I returned to our respective cabins, and we packed our bags. I remembered to take pictures of the inside of the boat. Buddy made sure everything was stowed properly. He, too, moved his belongings from his room to my cabin since it was the slightly larger of the two crew cabins. I took the towels and bed sheets to our bungalow because it had a washer and dryer. It would have taken twice as long in the combination washer and dryer on the boat. I swept and mopped the floor in the salon. Tyler volunteered to clean the smaller bathroom. Buddy took care of cleaning the owner's suite.

We completed the work about mid-afternoon. "Time for some lunch," Buddy said. "I think the Hodos is ready for Harvey and Carol."

We decided to go to the marina restaurant for our last lunch on the island. We placed our orders and chatted for a while.

"What do you think about putting up some decorations for Carol's retirement?" I asked. "The grocery store might have a party goods section."

Buddy said, "I think Carol would like that. See what you can find."

After lunch, Tyler and Buddy walked back to the guest house and I walked the short distance to the grocery store. They had a section of potted plants, floral arrangements, balloons and helium. I selected a "Happy Retirement" mylar balloon and a floral arrangement.

When I returned to the room, Buddy and Tyler were watching TV. I showed them my purchase, and they approved. Once the linens were dry, we went back to the boat, made the beds; and I set the arrangement - with the balloon attached - on the table in the salon. Before leaving the boat, I asked Buddy, "Will you take a picture of Tyler and me beside the boat?"

"Certainly." Buddy took my cell phone and snapped a couple of shots for me.

There were some people on a boat beside us. I asked the lady if she would take a picture of all three of us. She was happy to do so.

"What can we do for the rest of our last day at Spanish Wells?" I asked.

Buddy replied, "I know where we can go - to the Glass Window Bridge."

"Where is that?" I asked.

"It is on the north end of Eleuthera - about 15 miles away."

"How do we get there?" Tyler asked.

"We can get a local taxi to take us there," Buddy replied. "We need to walk over there before the last taxi leaves."

It did not take long to walk to the gas docks. The local taxis were next door. The route was quite scenic. There was one road from Spanish Wells to Gregory Town. When we reached our destination, the bridge traversed across a mountain of rock formations that is referred to as the narrowest place on earth. On one side, the blue waters of the Atlantic Ocean crash onto the rocks. On the other side, the calmer Bight of Eleuthera and its clear turquoise water can be seen. Under the bridge, the two bodies of water merge over the rocks beneath.

Just down the road was an area called the Queen's Bath, with natural pools of water made by erosion of the rocky shore of the Atlantic Ocean over the years. The water in the shallow pools warms from the sun. These tide pools flourish with seashells after high tide. The sun was lowering into the horizon, indicating it was time for us to return to Spanish Wells.

"This was a splendid idea, Buddy!" Tyler exclaimed, "I've never seen anything like these places."

I added, "What a wonderful way to end our stay here. Thank you."

Buddy said, "It was my pleasure."

I nodded off on the ride back, placing my head on Tyler's shoulder. He put his arm around me and fell asleep as well.

We both awoke when the taxi stopped at its destination.

Ambling back to our lodging, we stopped at a small restaurant on South Street. Since it was our last night on the islands, I ordered lobster pasta and a conch fritter. Tyler selected two Mahi-Mahi tacos, and Buddy enjoyed his usual seafood platter.

After dinner, we walked back to our rooms. Since I slept on the sofa bed in the living area, I had to wait for Tyler and Buddy to turn in for the night before I could go to sleep. It had been a busy day, and we were all exhausted.

CHAPTER 43

Surprises!

arvey and Carol were scheduled to come in on the early bird flight. The North Eleuthera Airport was only about seven miles from Spanish Wells. We were having coffee and bagels when Harvey called Buddy to let him know they had arrived. Buddy said, "They will be here in about 20 minutes. Carol thinks they are staying at Spanish Wells to celebrate her retirement, and she thinks I am vacationing here. Since Carol hasn't met you, I want you to go to the boat and wait for us there."

"When does our flight leave today?" I asked.

"Later this afternoon. Harvey is bringing your tickets with him."

After cleaning the kitchen, I packed my bags and checked under the couch and in the bathroom to make sure I had not left any articles. Tyler and Buddy were gathering their stuff together as well. We had just placed the luggage next to the door and walked to the dock. While we were boarding the Hodos, we heard a car drive up.

"We got here just in time," I said. "Where should we sit?"

"Since Carol will see the balloons and arrangement on the table when she comes in the door, let's sit on the couch in the salon."

"Yea, she will know something is up."

We looked out the window and saw Harvey and Carol knock on the door. Buddy came out to greet them and showed them into the apartment. A few minutes later, they walked together down the ramp. Apparently, Harvey still had not told her anything because they were looking at all the boats docked in the marina. They stopped at the Hodos. I heard Harvey say, "That is a nice catamaran. I wonder if anyone is onboard? I'd love to see inside."

Buddy said, "I'll check and see." Buddy entered the cockpit and knocked on the door. We played along. Tyler opened the salon door and said, "Hello, sir. Can I help you?"

Buddy replied, "We were admiring your boat. May we have permission to come aboard and look around?"

"Certainly. Welcome aboard!"

Buddy helped Carol step down into the cockpit, and Harvey followed. Tyler stood at the door and showed them inside. "What is this, Harvey?" Carol asked.

"It looks like a flower arrangement with a balloon that says, Happy Retirement," Harvey replied.

She eyed Tyler and Aspen. "I know that, but how did these young people know? What is going on, Harvey?" she asked perplexingly.

"Carol, let me introduce you to Aspen Blair and Tyler Dent."

Carol smiled and said, "Pleased to meet you."

We smiled and returned a greeting.

"How do you know them, Harvey?"

Harvey responded, "Aspen and Tyler are crew for Buddy. They sailed the boat from St. Marys, Georgia to Spanish Wells."

She turned to Buddy, "This is your yacht?"

Harvey declared, "Carol, this is our yacht. Happy Retirement!"

Carol put her hands to her face and cried out, "I can't believe it! I am speechless!" She turned and hugged Harvey and gave him a kiss. "I thought we were going to vacation here."

"We are going on a vacation, starting in Spanish Wells. Buddy has agreed to teach me all about the boat while we sail to Georgetown, Exuma. Buddy, will you give us a tour?"

Buddy showed us around the boat - in the same manner as he did for us at St. Marys. We moved to the cockpit and sat there while they looked around the boat. Buddy escorted Harvey and Carol to the cockpit and took the topside to the flybridge.

"I think Carol is happy with the catamaran," I surmised.

Tyler added, "I think she and Harvey will do fine."

The happy couple and Buddy came back to the cockpit and sat across from us.

Harvey said, "Buddy tells me you two did a great job."

I said, "Buddy is a fantastic teacher."

"We got along very well together," Tyler responded.

Harvey said, "I want to take all of you to lunch. Let's walk over to the marina restaurant."

Carl and Harvey followed Buddy and us. The weather was comfortable for eating lunch on the deck. We ordered our choices. Harvey gave thanks for our meal, fellowship and safe travel.

After lunch, we walked back to the guest house. Harvey handed us our plane tickets. "I've arranged for you to be picked up soon. Your flight leaves in two hours." He handed us one envelope each. "Here is the rest of your payment for crewing with Buddy. I couldn't have made a better choice."

"Thank you, Harvey," I replied. "I will never forget this experience."

Tyler shook Harvey's hand and said, "Thank you for allowing me this opportunity."

We gathered our bags, went outside and waited for our ride.

Buddy walked out with us. "I can never thank you enough for working with me and for your Christian witness."

"If you are ever in Atlanta, give us a call. We would love to keep up with you," I replied.

"Will do."

The taxi drove into the parking lot. "The driver loaded our bags into the trunk as we got into the car. We waved to Buddy, and he waved back. Soon we would be at the airport. I was sad that we were leaving; but I had to finish college, and Tyler needed to get back to work at the museum. We arrived at the airport, and the driver unloaded our luggage and directed us where to check in our bags.

The airport had internet, and I emailed my mom the time we expected to arrive in Atlanta so that they would be there to pick me up. I asked her if they would take Tyler to his apartment, so he wouldn't have to take a taxi. It would take them about two hours to drive to the airport from

Gainesville, which was about the length of our flight.

We boarded the plane without difficulty. Harvey had provided us with first-class seats. I asked Tyler, "What was your favorite island?"

He said, "That's a difficult question." He thought for a few minutes, "Great Guana Cay."

"We had a lot of fun there. How about your favorite island?"

"Spanish Wells. That is where you told me you loved me," I said.

Tyler said, "I liked Marsh Harbor as well. There were a variety of shops there."

"What was your favorite store?"

Tyler put his hand in his jacket pocket and pulled out a small box. "The store where I bought this for you." He opened the box. It had a small case inside of it. He opened it. "Will you marry me?"

Inside was a beautiful diamond ring. I was shocked! I looked at him and smiled, "Yes!"

I held my left hand, and he placed the ring on my finger. "It fits perfectly! How did you know my size?"

One day you were taking the towels out of the dryer, and one was frayed. I saw you twist the loose string with your finger and had trouble releasing it. I helped you get the string off but managed to maintain the size of the loop of string that had been on your ring finger. I traced the loop on a piece of paper and gave it to the jeweler."

"That's amazing!" I said.

"You are amazing," Tyler responded. Then we hugged and kissed each other.

"I'll want to finish college first before we get married. I hope you don't mind a long engagement."

"We will wait for God's timing," Tyler replied.

We talked about our future goals together until it was time to land in Atlanta. We disembarked from the plane, retrieved our luggage and went to the area where my parents were waiting.

"Aspen! How good it is to see you!" Mom exclaimed.

Dad greeted Tyler, and they shook hands.

"Mom, Dad, we have news. Tyler proposed to me on the plane. We're engaged!"

"Congratulations!" Mom said.

"That's wonderful news!" Dad added.

Dad dropped Tyler off at his apartment in Decatur, and then we drove to our home in Gainesville. "I have so much to tell you about my experience on the catamaran, but let's wait until tomorrow. I'm ready for bed."

Before falling asleep, I thought of all the wonderful things that God had done on this trip: Buddy's change of heart and Allen's conversion and baptism. But the best days were when Tyler told me he loved me and our engagement on the plane. I thanked God that He would guide us and direct our paths. The best was yet to come.

EPILOGUE

In 2010, my husband and I bought a 44-foot Lagoon Catamaran. Our itinerary included the Abaco Islands, Eleuthera and the Exuma Islands in the Bahamas - in hopes of sailing to Trinidad by way of the southernmost Caribbean islands. Our goal was to reach Rio de Janeiro, Brazil.

Our plans came to a halt at Little Farmer's Cay in the Exuma Islands when our mooring line came loose. We went aground on a rocky shore that tore a hole in one of the pontoons of our boat. After a temporary patch-up, we went to Spanish Wells in Eleuthera and the damage was permanently repaired. At that point, we decided that it was too much boat for us and we sold it.

I kept a journal, and this book is roughly based on our nine-week journey. Aspen Blair and Tyler Dent, from my first novel, The Spar Box, are the main characters.

In 2019, Hurricane Dorian ravaged the Abaco Islands by wind and storm surge, including Great Guana Cay, Elbow Cay and Green Turtle Cay. While researching online for this book in 2022, the islands we visited have been rebuilt and many of the establishments have reopened.

ACKNOWLEDGMENTS

The Orchards Gourmet
www.theorchardsgourmet.com

St. Marys Submarine Museum
www.stmaryssubmuseum.com

Naval Submarine Base Kings Bay
www.cnic.navy.mil/kingsbay

St. Augustine Municipal Marina
citystaug.com/798/Municipal-Marina

Fort Pierce City Marina
cityoffortpierce.com/1015/City-Marina

Elbow Reef Lighthouse, Hopetown, Elbow Cay, Abaco
https://www.elbowreeflighthousesociety.com

Captain Jack's Restaurant, Hopetown, Elbow Cay, Abaco
https://capnjackshopetown.com

Farmer's Cay Yacht Club and Marina, Little Farmer's Cay, Exuma
https://www.farmerscayyachtclub.com

R & B Boatyard, Spanish Wells, Eleuthera
www.rbboatyard.com

www.ingramcontent.com/pod-product-compliance
Lightning Source LLC
Chambersburg PA
CBHW061515120726
48001CB00004B/1324